WICKED GAMES

A COLLEGE BULLY ROMANCE

HIDDEN VALLEY ELITE SERIES
BOOK SEVEN

ISLA VAUGHN

ARROWSCOPE PRESS, LLC

CHAPTER ONE

SHANE

I couldn't shake the ominous feeling when Erica messaged about class letting out early. As her bodyguard, I was supposed to keep her safe. I raced across campus to her location and pushed aside all thoughts except getting to her.

I slipped through the breezeway and wove through students exiting, and as I rounded the back of the building, I saw red. Erica's ex—Luke Green—had her pinned against the brick, roughly kissing her. She struggled then managed to turn her head and cry out as my hand clamped on his shoulder.

He was an inch taller than me, but that didn't matter. Brown hair cropped short, a lean but muscular build, and an entitled chip on his shoulder. His family had money. He thought he was untouchable. The reports Erica had filed against him had gone unresolved, so her parents had hired me to keep her safe.

A sneer curved Luke's lips, and I matched it.

"Go away, Luke!" Erica shouted. "I don't want anything to do with you anymore. We're over."

"You heard her." I moved left, sweeping Erica behind me while herding Luke back a few inches. "Walk away."

"I don't think so." Luke tensed, his face an ugly mask of outrage.

He shifted his weight, and I saw the punch coming before he wound his arm back. I ducked, and his fist sailed past my head. I was done. He'd been asking for it for too damn long. Curling my hand, I put power behind my fist as it connected with his jaw.

The force of the hit jolted his head back as his eyes rolled into his head. His body followed, losing the ability to hold him upright. I stepped back as Luke went down. *Fuck.* I saw it too late. He hit the corner of a cement step. A dull thump echoed through the building pass-through, followed by Erica's scream.

Bile climbed my throat. *I should've grabbed him.* But I hadn't. And as he lay there, his head at an awkward angle against the cement step, blood pooled beneath him. Fluid leaked from his nose and ears. I knew what damage I'd done, how his skull must've cracked from impact on the corner. The sound played on a loop in my mind.

Erica pressed against my back. Her body convulsed, and her ear-piercing scream dissolved into sobs. I gathered her in my arms, blocking her view of Luke as I fumbled for my phone. Once I had it out of my pocket, I called 911 and, after that, campus security.

Students trickled in our direction. I yelled out that an ambulance was coming and to stay back. Erica's tears soaked my shirt. I held her tightly. She would've crumpled to the ground if I'd loosened my grip.

I couldn't not look at Luke. His chest wasn't moving. The fluid pooling beneath him grew. The minutes slowly ticked by, and I wished for a do-over, but nothing would change the fact that, today, I'd punched Luke Green—*once*. The power behind my fist as it made contact with his jaw had knocked him out cold, and he'd hit the ground, never to wake again.

I'd killed someone. Involuntary manslaughter. I couldn't

white-knuckle my way through it.

"What's going on—oh, shit." Campus security had arrived.

"An ambulance is coming." I didn't need to tell them.

The sirens grew louder the closer they came.

One of the guys lifted a radio and directed whoever was on the other end where to send the ambulance. The other guard got to work moving people back. My body was cold. I wasn't sure what would happen.

Luke Green's parents were heavy hitters at Thane University. They donated tons of money, and it was why Erica's complaints against him hadn't been handled. I had little hope that his parents would leave me be. They would come after me with everything they had when they discovered what had happened. And a part of me couldn't blame them.

Erica's sobs eased, but her trembling did not, and I worried she was in shock. As security pushed back the gathering crowd, Erica and I moved to an area where onlookers could not film us.

I read one of the campus security guy's name tags—Robert Fredrickson. He seemed to be the most take-charge one of the three on scene. And once the scene was as controlled as possible, Robert approached. I was ready for him. I just hoped Erica was too.

"I'll need your names." He held a small notebook, his pen poised and ready. Then his eyes narrowed, and a wide smile curved his mouth. "Shane Bennett. Gerald Bennett and I go way back. He told me to watch out for his grandsons."

"Nice to meet you, sir."

"Quite a year you've had, even with the injury. Both you and your brother are breaking football records." Robert glanced back at the body and grimaced. "Unfortunate time to meet. All right, let's get the story." He turned to Erica. "And you are?"

"Erica Williams."

"You're also a student here?"

"Yes." Her voice trembled, and tears leaked from her eyes in a steady stream.

"And that is?" Robert's eyes snapped back to mine as he motioned to the body not far from where we stood.

"Luke Green." Erica's voice shook. "H-He attacked me."

I clenched my teeth, knowing her accusation could be misconstrued. But maybe not, as Robert was clearly a football fan.

"What do you mean? He hit you?"

"No. But he pushed me against the wall and kissed me. He wouldn't let me go. I told him to stop. I said no."

"And why are you here, Shane?"

He turned to me, dismissing Erica for the time being. I hadn't checked for cameras, but I hoped there were some. "The Williams family hired me to keep their daughter safe when she walked from classes to her car. Her ex-boyfriend"—I indicated Luke—"wouldn't take no for an answer and had been harassing her. Incidents have been filed with the university."

"If you were with her, why did Luke have the chance to make advances on her?"

He gave nothing away when he questioned me. I could do nothing but tell the truth and hope that, somehow, the tragedy would be seen as the accident it was. "Her class let out early. Erica messaged me about it and said she was going to her car. When I found them, I had to pull Luke off her. He took a swing at me, and I retaliated."

"You hit him repeatedly?"

"No. Once." But that had been all it took. One swing, and everything had changed in that second.

The ambulance arrived, and paramedics spilled from the vehicle. They bent to assess Luke and came to the same conclusion we all had. A squad car parked alongside the ambulance, just behind the path we would have been on to the parking lot if her ex hadn't intervened.

Two officers crowded around us, and we exchanged the

same information. When they realized I was on Thane's football team, their tone of questioning changed as it had with Robert. Erica backed me up, reiterating my story and that it was a horrible accident. We gave our contact information and were told we had to go to the police station to file a statement.

Erica's complexion was alarmingly pale. I got her to my SUV since she was in no shape to drive, then we went to the station. We gave our statements and were fingerprinted, processed for evidence, then told we were free to go, that it was a clear case of self-defense. I had to assure them we wouldn't leave town. I mentioned I would be at my mom's after dropping Erica off. It felt like a mistake, them letting me go, but I hoped I was wrong.

I ushered her out of the station and took her to her parents' house. We explained the altercation to them, and as I left, Erica called out to me.

"It wasn't your fault. It was self-defense."

Was it? I wasn't so sure. I had control. I could've stopped it— or at the very least stopped him from falling.

Not knowing what else to do, I went to Mom's house. I didn't remember the drive. Somehow, I was inside my mom's home, where I'd grown up, feeling lost. I'd killed someone.

"Shane." Mom rounded a corner from the back to find me standing in the foyer. "I wasn't expecting you." The happiness that had lit up her face melted away when she got a good look at me. "What's wrong?"

A wave of despair washed over me. I had to tell her. She would find out, and I would rather it be from me. So I did. Every detail—from being hired by Erica's family to what happened that day.

"It'll be okay. It's not your fault."

But she was shaken. I could tell. And she was wrong. It was my fault.

Being released and told I was free to go felt too good to be true. And I would soon find out that it was.

CHAPTER TWO

SHANE

In the back of my mind, I'd counted the minutes until they came for me—the police with their flashing lights painting the front of our house red and blue. I knew they would. Luke Green's family wouldn't accept the self-defense argument for their only child.

A witness had come forward, one produced by the Green family.

My world continued to crumble. As the police hauled me out of my mom's house in handcuffs, I jerked my head to the side when an SUV pulled up behind the squad cars in the drive. Phoenix and Aspen, his pregnant wife, got out.

"What's going on?"

Alarm laced my brother's question as Mom flew down the front steps. Her hand shook as she grabbed his forearm. It was the worst fucking day of my life. The tears and helplessness on my mom's face were etched into my mind.

After everything she's done for us, this is how I repay her?

The feel of the metal cuffs the police officer slapped on me stayed with me, a deep scar on my psyche I wasn't sure I would ever be able to purge. Nor could I shake the charge for the arrest ringing in my ears.

Shame and anguish swirled in my gut, threatening to crawl up my throat at the most inopportune time, like during finger-printing and having my mug shot taken.

I managed to swallow it down, but the guilt remained, something I didn't think would ever go away. My fingers, so tightly clenched, were devoid of color, of blood flow. The anxiety of being in the police station, cuffed then processed again, was a fucking nightmare. I didn't want to have a criminal record in common with my estranged dad, even if he'd been acquitted when it'd happened to him at a much younger age than my nineteen years.

The single call I was granted went to my uncle Lucas's law office. I requested the receptionist inform him of my predica-ment despite him being out of town with his wife and my being assigned a criminal defense lawyer by the state. My cousins, Cole and Damon, Uncle Lucas's sons, had found out by then. Mom had probably called Grandad, too, as if my life weren't already a clusterfuck.

The cop who took my information led me to a holding cell, removed the handcuffs, and slammed the bars shut, effectively locking me in. I had nothing but time and the horror of my thoughts.

Would this have happened if I hadn't taken the part-time body-guard job Erica Williams's family had hired me to do for the last six months? I wanted to say no, there was no way it would have. Probably not how Luke's death had played out at least, but possibly another way. I'd been informed he'd wanted to fight.

I sat on the cell's hard metal bench and worried for an entirely new reason. Luke knew of the underground fights I participated in and had set one up to go against me. I'd even told Snake, the guy who ran the fights, that Luke had no business fighting based on our conflicting interests outside the Ring. It was a massive risk that Luke had caught wind of them, and ultimately, the payout that could tie me to the fights. *Does that mean his parents know too? Will they find any documentation from Luke that could lead to me?*

Snake had assured me that all transactions were handwritten, not electronically recorded, and got destroyed at the end of the night. No record of any payouts or the names of the fighters remained. That wasn't the problem. Fighting wasn't illegal. The gambling was, and the payouts.

That was my next biggest fear, after being locked in a holding cell. If the police found evidence of illegal gambling, I could kiss my future—one I'd hoped would be in the NFL—and potentially my freedom, goodbye.

The NFL wasn't a sure thing, a fact my brother had capitalized on in a conversation to my at-the-time high school girlfriend of two years. And thanks to my brother's lie that my shoulder injury would be career ending, Tracey had promptly broken things off with me—in a text, the summer before our first year of college. The injury had happened during a pickup game at a barbecue thrown by the football house where we would soon live—and where Cole already lived at the time.

I'd been in a downward spiral ever since. College was a new playing field, and I'd taken advantage of sleeping my way through sorority girls, TAs, and even a professor to fill the loneliness and feelings of never being enough. Mistakes were made, but eventually, I regained some semblance of control.

The fights helped. They were like therapy for the turmoil and mass destruction my life became after my shoulder injury sidelined me. And after I healed, and even before I was back on Thane's football team, I'd been a regular fighter in the underground events to help pay the bills and take the edge off the restlessness that had me itching for a fight or sex.

Of the four of us—my two cousins and my twin—I was the only one still fighting in them. We'd fought in the Ring since our first year of high school, and that had transferred to college. Cole, a year older than the rest of us, had stopped when he started at Thane University. He considered it too big a risk to his chance at getting drafted into the NFL, and he worried it would taint his girlfriend's image during Riley's Olympic trial. Damon wasn't far behind. And my brother had quit this year, after a traumatic brain injury that had come on the heels of our grandad getting too involved in his life in the worst way.

The rest, recovery, and PT had been grueling. He'd had to live at home during the process, with all of us, including Aspen, checking up on him. But my brother was strong, his drive ingrained in every fiber of his being, and he'd exceeded the doctors' expected timelines, enabling him to move back to college after winter break.

I dropped my head into my hands. *When will the lawyer arrive and spring me from this place?* The timing was absolute shit. I didn't know if Uncle Lucas would get the message anytime soon. Being in there, with only my thoughts and the too-real sounds of the police station as company, was slowly driving me crazy.

I was fucking up my life, and I didn't know how to stop. I leaned back against the cold cinder block wall, my leg bouncing nervously as a temporary outlet for my out-of-control emotions. I alternated between sitting with restless energy and pacing my cell like a strung-out junkie jonesing for my next fix. Time elongated, and while I might only have been locked up a couple of hours, it felt like days.

It was so messed up. Saliva flooded my mouth, and I frantically swallowed against the nausea. I'd killed someone. Ended his life. I couldn't get that thought out of my head. Even if Luke had been asking for the hit, it never should've cost him his life.

What if that had been my brother or one of my cousins? Tears flooded my eyes, and I blinked them back, counting out each breath in a desperate attempt for something else to focus on and slow the panic attack that clawed at my throat. *I'm so screwed.*

An officer rounded the corner of the back holding cell hallway, his square face void of emotion.

I stood, my hands automatically curling around the cold steel bars. My skin crawled expectantly. *Is my lawyer here?*

"You have a visitor." His flat, almost monotone voice scratched over my eardrums.

I glanced at his name tag—not that knowing his name would do me any good—then I backed up so he could unlock my cell and lead me to a conference room at the end of the hall. A small window sat high on the tan metal door Officer Biaggio opened and held until I entered.

The deep growl was one I recognized instantly. *Not my lawyer.* My shoulders tensed more, if that was even possible.

Grandad stood with his back to the door. Salt-and-pepper hair, broad shoulders, and a height the same as mine at a couple of inches over six feet, he took up more space with his big personality than the room provided as he yelled into the phone pressed to his ear.

The cop grunted, but once I stepped inside, he shut the door behind me, trapping me with my irate grandad.

"I don't give a rat's ass if he called you first." Grandad was talking to Uncle Lucas. "Shane and Phoenix fall under my jurisdiction. Nothing has changed since my daughter took her life while under *your* care. We made an agreement while she was alive, and you *will* honor it."

Grandad was referring to Mom's sister, our aunt and Uncle Lucas's first wife—another tragedy that had happened a few years ago. *How much will I have to endure today?*

Silence followed, and I closed my eyes, tilted my face to the ceiling, and took a steadying breath. Grandad was ripping my uncle a new one because of me. I knew Uncle Lucas would want to help. He would move heaven and earth to do so, but Grandad was the primary force in our lives after Mom. He made it very clear that our uncle had no say or control regarding finances or if we needed help. Legalities fell under that category. I should have called Grandad, but Uncle Lucas would have swept in with a team of lawyers and made things go much smoother. I pulled out one of the metal chairs and took a seat.

"My lawyer is five minutes out. If we need anything, we will let you know." He hung up then turned to face me. "What the hell have you done?"

So, it would be like that. Accusations. Lectures. I wished Uncle Lucas had been in town and had arrived before Grandad. I loved Grandad, but he could be a lot to manage.

"Mom called you?"

"Yes." His lips pressed into a thin line, the grooves around his mouth deepening as he sat opposite me. "Who was the boy you hit and why?"

Christ. My chest tightened painfully. I didn't want to go over it again. But it wouldn't be the first time, and I would have to man up and do what I had to. "The kid's name is Luke Green, and he was messing with a girl I was hired to protect. He took a swing at me, so I hit back."

He'd already heard the story from Mom, and part of me wanted to call him out on it, but whatever. If I wanted to give more details, he was there to listen, and that was what he said without words.

"Self-defense. You'll be out of here within the hour." Grandad leaned back in his chair, and it creaked ominously.

"I don't think it's that simple." The Green family would be out for blood, despite their kid harassing a girl. "The charge is involuntary manslaughter. And it's why I called Uncle Lucas. I might need a team of lawyers, and he would have delivered that."

Grandad waved away the words that still felt like a noose around my neck. "I'll tell you what. If my lawyer thinks working with his is best, then we'll do that."

So generous of him. I kept my mouth shut. No matter the questionable things Grandad had done in the name of family, love, and loyalty, I owed him a certain amount of respect. And I knew he wouldn't let me down. We would need a team, and Grandad would see it that way eventually too.

He glanced at a text on his phone before training those world-weary eyes on me. "Before my lawyer gets here, we have a few minutes to discuss a call I got from the bank. You asked the bank about taking a loan out against the trust your nona and I set up for you? Would you like to explain that?"

Anger whipped through me like a riptide. "I'm doing my best to keep up with football, work, and manage my classes so that my partial scholarship isn't revoked and I can pay for classes without going to Mom for help." I resented the hell out of him for not helping, at least with tuition, and that was the reason I'd inquired about the trust Phoenix and I had only just learned about. I hadn't gone through with trying to take a loan out against it, but that bank manager must've had Grandad on speed dial. If I needed to, I could survive in a run-down apartment, pleading hardship to Coach so I could move out of the football house and make things easier on myself.

My brother had an almost full ride. He didn't have the struggles I did. Winning a fight here and there was enough to cover what he needed. It wasn't for me. The bodyguarding gig made up the rest of the money, not the internship Grandad had practically forced on me during my rare downtime. But that was gone.

"Care to explain about the fight you made Phoenix throw?"

"You'd better shut your mouth." Grandad leaned closer. "Accusations like that are dangerous."

"I call bullshit." *Like I wouldn't believe my twin on something like that? For the way he'd forced Phoenix to throw a fight, and worse, the way he'd tried to force Aspen to disappear from my brother's life?*

Grandad's face turned a mottled shade of red, and he leaned forward. "We aren't discussing Phoenix now, are we? You're in enough of a mess all on your own."

I clenched my fists under the table, where he couldn't see them. Grandad was nothing if not stubborn. And since I was the peacemaker of all my headstrong relatives, I let it go. "Fine. But if the lawyer agrees, I want Uncle Lucas's team involved. This is my future on the line, not your pride."

Weathered hands flattened on the table between us, and the usual ego that held Grandad rigid in his beliefs melted away. "Your best interests are all I care about. I'll tell my lawyer to involve Lucas's team regardless. It can't hurt, and the last thing I want is for you to face jail time and risk your NFL dreams."

We all had those dreams—Phoenix, Cole, Damon, and myself.

My shoulders dropped a full inch as the tension eased from them. "Thank you."

Grandad meant well. He just didn't always go about things the best way, like what he'd done to Phoenix, Aspen, and my parents. But those were issues for another day.

The door opened, and the same officer stood to the side while a tall, thin man with wire-rimmed glasses and a custom-made suit breezed inside. He shook hands with Grandad first then held out his palm to me.

"Frank Nicholson, please call me Frank."

I took his hand, noting his firm grip and brisk, get-down-to-business manner. "Shane Bennett."

He pulled out the metal chair next to Grandad, pushed up his glasses, then took a file from his briefcase. "A witness has come forward, and the police made a mistake releasing you too early, from what I've been told. Are you aware of the charges brought against you and what they mean?"

"Yes." I didn't need to repeat the words branded in my mind.

"Before we begin," Grandad interrupted, "Shane would like his uncle's lawyers to join you in representation."

"I have no problem with that." Frank gave Grandad a curt nod. "I'm on good terms with several legal associates who work for Lucas Savage. I'll convene with them after our meeting." Then he gave me his undivided attention. "Everything we discuss here is protected under attorney-client privilege. With that being said, I need to know everything that led up to and resulted in the death of Lucas Green."

The level of confidence Frank wielded fueled my resolve to share what had happened with him in the hopes that he could get all charges dropped. "Erica Williams's family hired me to act as a bodyguard for her during certain times of the day, basically after her classes and escorting her safely to her car." It was easy money and worked with my schedule.

"What made her family seek you out? Why did they think you were qualified to be a bodyguard?"

That was the tricky part. "She told her parents about me after seeing me in a fight."

"And what fight was that?"

"An underground one." I clenched my jaw so hard I was surprised my teeth didn't fracture on the spot. I'd just admitted to doing something that could get me in a world of trouble.

Frank's face held no judgment. "Why did she choose you and not one of the other fighters?"

"Most of the other ones she knew of were 'wifed up.' The guys that weren't didn't have my win-to-loss record. She thought I would be the least complicated option, as I have no girlfriend involved."

"Why did she need a bodyguard?"

"Erica used to date Luke. When she broke up with him, he didn't take it well. When he cornered her one too many times, she and her parents got worried."

"Why not report the guy to campus security?"

I smirked. "They did, but Luke Green's family has connections. They're the kind of wealthy that colleges salivate over. They're the most significant benefactors at Thane University."

"Tell me about the confrontation."

"Erica's last class ended early today. She texted me about it. I replied that I was on my way, but she said she would head to her car and thought it would be all right. When I arrived, Luke had her pinned against the back of a building near a rear entrance. She was crying."

"How far did he take things?"

I shrugged. "He kissed her. Maybe groped her some, but nothing past that. He only had her trapped there for a few seconds before I found them because Erica shared her location with me on her phone."

When I paused, Frank nodded for me to continue.

What came next was the hard part. "I pulled Luke off her, and he took a swing, which I ducked. Then I punched him. He went down. He landed on a concrete step—the corner of it, which must've damaged his skull—and his head fell at an awkward angle. Maybe he snapped his neck."

"Did you know he was dead?"

"I suspected, but I didn't know. It all happened so fast. He looked wrong when he fell, but Erica was freaked out."

"Who called 911?"

"I did."

"Is there anything else?"

"No, sir. I explained everything to campus security and the police officers who arrived with the ambulance. We gave our statement at the police station, and when they said I was free to go, we left. I took Erica to her parents' and went to my mom's. That's when the police arrested me."

"I'm going to make some calls," Frank said. "It was self-defense, and after campus security releases the video from behind the building, we'll prove the witness wrong. For now, sit tight. I should be able to get you out of here within the hour."

"Thanks." I didn't have much choice but to do as he said. *Where else could I go?*

CHAPTER THREE

WINTER

The coastal town of Santa Monica should be a welcome sight. And to most, I'm sure it was. But my experiences there weren't like everyone else's. They were the stuff of nightmares. I dropped my head against the steering wheel of my parked car with a thump, shutting out the view of Thane University's brick-lined walkways, complete with historic architecture and lush greenery. It was hard to believe I was back, or relatively near, where it all began—and I mean *all*.

Where my dad died.

Where my sister was murdered.

Where my mom was arrested and sentenced to jail time.

None of those reasons were why I was back in town. I popped open my car door and unfurled from the aging Toyota my foster parents had gifted me for getting into Thane University. I didn't even remember applying. When the letter had come, I'd almost thrown it away, but then Brooke, my foster mom, had urged me to open it. She'd said it might contain an option I didn't know I had. And it certainly had.

Thane University's scholarship committee had read my sob story in the form of an essay and had taken pity on me. I wasn't too prideful to accept the offer, even if it meant leaving the safe haven the Childress family had provided in Los Angeles for the unknown that I would face in a hometown that had never wanted me in the first place.

Gathering my long wavy hair, I secured it in a messy knot on top of my head with a hair band from my wrist. I hadn't told my foster brother, Jaxon, that I would be arriving yet. Brooke and James knew, but I'd mentioned contacting Jaxon and had declined their help. It was ridiculous, but I wasn't sure how I would feel coming back.

Pain and a terrible hollowness at the memories spread through me, eating away what was left. *God, I miss Summer.* Facing that was something I needed to do alone. I could lean on Jaxon later, but I had to process the emotions surrounding my return to an area not too far from where my life had imploded so many times.

Palm fronds stirred overhead from the warm breeze. My feet grew roots as I wrestled with my shifting emotions. I flattened my hand against my stomach. I wasn't the same mean girl I had been after my mom had killed my sister, Summer. My behavior had defined me back then, though I shouldn't have let it. But I hadn't known how to deal with everything, so I'd lashed out.

I hadn't realized that I was the one everyone feared. Nor had I realized how hard a tumble would be from my precarious position, back then or even a few weeks ago. Not until I was lying on my back with the wind knocked out of me as my life played out on the TV.

One slow blink, and I shook myself out of my pity party, grabbed the oversized bag that held my purse, favorite art supplies, and the dreaded shoebox full of letters, and looped it over my shoulder. Car door slammed and locked, I pointed myself in the direction of the administration building where I was to meet someone who would take me to my new dorm room.

I slipped my keys into my shorts pocket and followed the sidewalk to the front door. An older woman sat behind the desk, chatting on the phone. She smiled and held up a finger, indicating that she would be a minute. I nodded in response then let my gaze bounce around the well-lit room. Light spilled in through oversized windows and bounced off the glossy wood and coffee tables in the ample seating beyond the reception desk. A door to the left and on the opposite wall must lead to advisor offices, but I would deal with that later, as I already had my schedule.

The click from the receiver returning to its base snapped my focus back to the woman in front of me.

"How can I help you?"

"I'm Winter Patten, a new student."

"Are you transferring?" She turned to face her monitor in the middle of her question and typed my name into the computer.

"Yes. I had a semester at a community college in Los Angeles."

Jaxon had been ready to leave home and go away to college. I had struggled with it, and Brooke and James had suggested a semester living at home and going nearby.

"Ah, yes. I've got your welcome packet right here." After another couple of clicks on her computer, she thumbed through a few manila envelopes until she came across one with my name scrawled across the top in black ink. "Let me just call Vanessa. She'll show you to your dorm."

"Oh, that's okay. I'm familiar with the campus."

"Are you sure, dear?"

"Yes. I'll be fine." I plastered a smile on that I didn't quite feel.

It must have worked, because she pulled out a map printed on a piece of white copy paper and, with a highlighter, drew the path I would need to take to get to my new living quarters.

"Your new roommate's name is in there as well. If you need anything"—she circled a number on the bottom right of the paper—"just call me. Welcome to Thane University, Winter."

"Thank you." I forced a smile then took the information from her outstretched hand.

A quick stop at my car and I pulled the huge suitcases out. Brooke had shoved my pillow, sheets, and blankets into a vacuum storage bag to maximize space so I didn't have to bring in a ton of stuff. As it was, I only had the one bag over my shoulder and two pieces of luggage on wheels.

It was a bit cumbersome, but I managed to maneuver both onto the sidewalk and to the place I would call home for the next semester. When I got to room 306 and opened the door, I stopped.

My roommate sat on her bed and look back at me.

My jaw dropped. "Piper?" Despite how much she'd changed, I still recognized her.

A wide smile stretched across Piper's face. She'd been beautiful when I knew her—we were best friends. Well, she was Summer's friend first, which meant she was mine too. Everything had changed, except for how stunning she looked when she smiled. I wondered if Piper was still the same.

She and I had been cut from a similar cloth back in the day. We'd both toed the line of "cut a bitch" if anyone crossed us. Her for reasons I wasn't all too familiar with. I remember her crying once about her parents fighting, so I guessed her aggression had come from her family.

It figured. My family had molded me into something I didn't like. As had my grandparents, who'd reluctantly taken me in for a few months, all the while telling me how unwanted I was. Nothing but a financial burden.

On a downward spiral, I had been dumped at child services when my grandparents had had enough of me. The sense of abandonment was overwhelming. Then the Childress family intervened and took me in. They taught me what a family should be like. They showed me love. Something that I'd only had with my sister, and we had been so young, those memories hadn't been able to sustain me or stop the darkness from spilling from me and onto others.

"Winter Patten." Piper crossed her arms and leaned a hip against her lofted bed. "I couldn't believe it when housing emailed me my new roommate's name." Her eyes flashed with emotion before she blinked the tears away.

I saw the pity before she managed to hide it. I hated it, but it was also the reason I was enrolled as a student at Thane. The essay, originally written for the therapist Brooke and James had set me up with and I'd seen on the regular, would have evoked an ocean's worth of god-awful emotion.

"Surprise." I forced a smile that I knew wouldn't reach my eyes. I, too, would have known about her had I cared enough to read the details in my packet past the room number. I waved to the bare mattress opposite hers. "I'm gonna unpack, but do you want to grab coffee? I've got a killer headache from lack of caffeine."

"Sure." Piper pointed to the suitcases, her long, shiny hair spilling over her shoulder. "I'll help. Give me the one with your clothes, and I can put them away."

I almost sagged in relief. I wanted to be done, like, yesterday. "Great. Thanks." I pushed that bag in her direction, set my oversized satchel on the desk, then unzipped the luggage that held my bedding, toiletries, and everything else. I didn't need much.

Most of the stuff I'd brought was because Brooke had insisted. She hated that I was moving in without their family being a part of it, but I needed to do it alone. And when she'd enveloped me in that last hug—hers were incomparable and something I deeply cherished—I knew she understood.

It didn't take me long to make the bed with the cool blue-gray sheets, stow my toiletries, hang a towel in the Jack-and-Jill bathroom we shared with another room, and put away my laptop and desk supplies. I shoved the empty suitcases under the bed and withdrew my purse from the oversized bag. Then I reluctantly set the shoebox Brooke had handed me on the top of my bed and waited for Piper to put on her shoes.

I took a second to sweep the room visually. Her side was an explosion of pink and silver. She'd always liked those colors, and nothing had changed there. But she had an air about her that was entirely different, and I couldn't place what it was just yet. Hopefully, I would figure it out when we caught up over much needed coffee.

My purse slipped off my shoulder, and as I bent to pick it up, my elbow snagged the corner of the shoebox. The box tumbled off the bed. Raw panic washed over me as the unopened letters from Mom scattered across the floor, banded together by year. Each bundle contained twelve letters, one for every month, from the last eight years.

We bent at the same time, gathering the bundles and stuffing them back into the box.

Piper picked up a stack and turned it over in her hand, the California State Penitentiary stamped on the upper-left corner as clear as day.

"Why haven't you opened these?" Her voice was gentle, but I still felt too exposed. "Maybe they contain something you'll want to know. The trial was a big deal."

Of course, it was. It wasn't like I hadn't been there. I was a witness. "My mom has nothing to say that I want to hear." My voice sounded strange, robotic almost. "I hope she dies in prison."

I meant it, too, and by Piper's raised eyebrows, I would assume she registered the truth in my words. I grabbed the letters from her hand, shoved them back in the box, then stashed them under my bed. Out of sight, out of mind.

But Mom wasn't. She'd been sentenced to ten years in prison

for manslaughter, and only two remained on her sentence. It wasn't nearly long enough.

"Let's get out of here." I adjusted my purse strap on my shoulder to secure it, pocketing the new key to the space I would call home for the next semester.

"Sure." Piper wisely dropped the topic, and we swept out of the room then the dorm.

Outside, we walked the handful of blocks to the Spot. It was a local coffee shop popular with Thane U's students. Or that was what she said.

When we arrived, I breathed in the rich aroma, wishing I could infuse it into my veins. We placed our orders and got lucky when two girls got up from their table, tossing their empty to-go cups in the trash on their way out. We grabbed the table before someone else could.

"Is it always this packed?" I asked.

She shrugged then took a sip of her caramel macchiato. "Pretty much."

"Since it's been years—"

"Eight."

"Right. What I was trying to ask"—I flashed a small smile to soften my words—"was, what've you been up to? You seem… different."

A perfectly sculpted brow arched above her sky-blue eyes. "Aren't we all? It's been ages, Winter."

"That's true."

"You seem different too. So maybe we should take things slow?"

I pushed out a breath before answering. "Sounds good." I tapped my nail on the shiny wooden tabletop. "Do you like it here? At Thane, I mean?"

Her face softened, and the guarded expression she'd worn since I'd started my awkward questions melted away. "Yeah, it's pretty great. There are so many people. It's not like high school."

A mocking chuckle fell from her lips. "And I'm glad for that. I'm majoring in architecture with a minor in business, and I've never been busier. It's…" She looked to the ceiling as if the words would fall from above. "What I'm meant to do, but it requires a crazy amount of work and time."

"No more cheerleading?" She'd been involved in the peewee leagues when we were small.

"I thought about it but decided it wasn't the direction I wanted to go. This is sort of like a fresh start, though a ton of people from Hidden Valley Academy go here."

I crossed my legs, my foot hooking around one of the dark metal poles of the table. The coffee shop had such a great atmosphere. I could see myself doing homework or sketching with copious amounts of coffee over the semester. I glanced at the counter and the sugary goodness behind the glass. Coffee wouldn't be my only treat.

Before I could turn back toward Piper, my gaze snagged on a guy placing his order at the register. His shoulders were impossibly wide, the muscles bunching and shifting under the light-gray Henley. His body screamed athlete, and I couldn't help but wonder which sport as I visually traced the V of his back to a tapered waist and thick, muscular thighs. His dark, almost black hair was cropped short on the sides and a little longer on top.

Come on. Turn.

I wanted to see if he was as mouth-watering from the front as he was at that angle. Then he did, and I choked as I tried to swallow. Turning my mouth into my elbow, I coughed before clearing my throat. Eyes watering, I lifted them, and they collided with his stormy-blue ones.

Piper had gone silent, but I wouldn't have heard her while caught in his sight. The room shrank, and I could only focus on his chiseled, model-worthy face. Some familiarity in his features tickled the back of my mind, but I couldn't place him. He was athletic, gorgeous, and with a commanding air that screamed unforgettable.

"You need to stay away from that guy."

Piper's sharp voice cut through the fantasy I had going with the mystery man, and I shifted in my seat. Released from the most intense eye contact I'd ever experience, I watched the room flood back into my vision, as did the low hum of conversation around me. Piper's lips pressed together, and she looked uncomfortable as she stood beside our table.

When did she get up? "Are you leaving?"

With her coffee and keys in hand, she nodded. "I have class in about fifteen minutes. The bookstore is on the way. If you want to leave with me, we can walk there together."

"Yeah, let's do that."

Her gaze narrowed as she probably noted that I hadn't successfully been warned off that guy.

"I mean it. Stay away from him. I heard his last fight didn't end favorably for his opponent."

I swung my gaze back to the tall, good-looking guy. I couldn't get him out of my mind if I tried. He didn't look dangerous. Maybe it was the masochist in me, but I could see myself liking him. And by how he'd made me feel with one look, staying away wasn't an option, regardless of Piper's warning.

He stood to the side of the counter where orders were placed, chatting with another athletic-looking guy whose face was turned from me. Ideas sifted through my mind. Maybe I could run into my mystery man by accident a few times until he got the idea that those run-ins weren't coincidence. A slow smile curved my lips. I bet I could convince him that there were better things to do with his hands than fight. Things had just gotten interesting. With a visual of that guy, I had plenty of material to sustain me through the night.

And on that delicious thought, I picked up my coffee and

joined Piper as we pushed through the door, heading toward the campus bookstore.

"If he's so dangerous, why is he walking free and not behind bars?"

"I don't know what to tell you, but Luke Green is dead because of that man."

CHAPTER FOUR

SHANE

It was the worst week of my life. And if Phoenix hadn't dragged me to the Spot for coffee, I would've stayed in my room and done homework. That was all I could manage lately—football, class, homework. Rinse and repeat. The whispers as I walked by were more annoying than anything. *But why deal with them if I don't have to?*

My brother stood to the side, as he'd already placed his order. And when I turned, I froze at the sight of the willowy strawberry blonde staring right at me.

Winter Patten.

I couldn't fucking believe it was her. The girl who had made my entire fifth grade miserable in ways I couldn't believe I'd survived. She'd made me question my existence, and I would never forgive her.

She'd treated me like shit, had hated me, and I'd had the biggest crush on her. She made school so terrible that I'd faked countless illnesses. The names she'd called me back then rang in my ears, and I clenched my jaw against the memories.

It got so bad that my mom had called hers after she'd managed to pry some of what was happening out of me. Of course, our moms talking backfired. When Winter had told me she was sorry and to meet her behind the dugout on the baseball field, that we could kiss and make up, I'd believed her. I'd even been stupid enough to let her blindfold me. When I'd puckered my lips, someone had snapped a picture. The laughter had alerted me to the problem. She'd shared that damn picture everywhere.

I had thought I'd left all that angst and anxiety behind, but two seconds after seeing her, I struggled to speak normally. The sense of losing control, the tightness around my mouth, and the spike in my distress were acute.

I squared my shoulders and held her gaze. I wasn't the same person as that insecure kid. A football star, I kicked ass with my eyes fucking closed. I did not cower. I did not hide. And I damn well would not revert to childhood stuttering.

Phoenix smacked my shoulder, making my head swivel back to face him and away from the redheaded devil.

"How long do you have to work with Grandad to compensate for the lawyer's fees?"

I took a deep breath and forced the muscles around my mouth to relax. "I don't know. He said it wasn't about the money but the lesson. He'll cut me loose when he thinks I've sufficiently paid my dues."

I wanted to say it was bullshit, especially when I'd told him how hard I had to work to make ends meet and maintain all my respective responsibilities. But I couldn't. He wanted me to learn that if I wanted something, I had to work for it. My punishment might have held another meaning, but that was the one I took from it.

"I can't believe that happened." Phoenix sipped his coffee as the barista finally called my name.

I retrieved my drink from the counter then joined my brother at the table he managed to grab while I got my drink. "I'm just glad the charges were dropped after the security video backed me up on what I'd told them." *But if the Greens get wind of the underground fights, could they use that to reopen the case against me?* I didn't know. To be safe, I'd told Snake I couldn't revisit any locations Luke had known about. The risk was too significant.

And after, Uncle Lucas had cornered me and made me promise no more fights. I'd agreed. At least I wouldn't be duking it out in the prison yard, so I made peace with saying goodbye to it altogether.

A visual sweep around the room revealed that Winter had left, and the remaining tension along the back of my neck eased. "Do you remember Winter Patten?"

Phoenix nodded, his silver eyes, like our dad's, darkened dangerously. He had been with me at the worst of it when she'd tormented me badly enough that I'd written a suicide note and planned to end myself.

At my brother's heated look, I chose not to elaborate and tell him she was back in town. "How's Aspen?"

"Sick of being pregnant." Phoenix grinned, the darkness fading at the mention of his wife. "I'm taking her to the beach for a weekend away."

"Not to surf." I didn't ask it as a question because it scared the hell out of me that she'd done so for as long as she had. Too much could happen, no matter how good or careful she was.

"No. She just needs to be there. Soak it up. Since we're in the off-season and I have more time, I thought it would be good."

"She's got, what, another month to go?"

"Two, unless the baby comes early. Then a month and a half." He ran his hand through his blond hair. "It'll be the shorter of the two if she has her way."

"It's going to be so weird, you having a baby. I still can't wrap my head around you being married, even if Aspen is pretty great."

Phoenix smacked the side of my head, and I laughed. I hadn't always thought that about her. Things changed, and she'd become one of us. I didn't need to say it. He knew. As twins, we had a different kind of connection. We may not look alike. I took after Mom's dark hair and blue eyes, while Phoenix was blond with silver eyes, just like our dad. But none of that mattered. I could feel emotions swirling off him in a tangible sense. It wasn't telepathy or anything like that, but we were in tune with what the other thought or felt, so it amazed me that I hadn't known about his lie to Tracey when it'd happened. Then again, I didn't think I'd wanted to.

"You still screwing that professor?"

"Cindy?"

"First names, huh? I guess that answers my question. I'm glad it's not the same art professor Aspen has."

"Yeah, I have zero interest in Professor Potts." I couldn't stop the shudder that tore through me. "Cindy is insane in the sack, but I'm done with her." She was crazy and would not go away.

"Probably for the best. You're not thinking about getting back with Tracey, are you?"

I knew he still felt guilty about destroying that relationship for me, though in the end, it seemed he'd had Tracey pegged better than I had. He wanted me to find someone like Aspen, but that might not be in the cards for me.

"No. I think you were right about her." It was as close as I could come to telling him I forgave him for his lie, and I knew he would understand.

"Yeah, but it still sucks."

His words were quiet, but the way his shoulders relaxed told me he'd needed to hear them.

"Mom probably wouldn't mind if you could stop by," Phoenix said.

Guilt hit me like a sledgehammer to the gut. I'd put her through so much in the last week. "I'll make a point of it." My lips curled in a self-deprecating grin. "I have more time, anyway, since my bodyguarding job is over as well as my Friday night fights."

Phoenix grimaced then set his coffee down and leaned his forearm on the table. "That's some shitty bad luck."

"Yeah, it couldn't have gone worse than it did. If I'd known what would've happened… But I didn't, and I need the money. I'm going to have to find something else."

"Aspen might need help with her business. Maybe shipping? I don't know how much she can pay, though."

I rapped my knuckles on the table and grabbed my to-go cup of coffee. "It's all right. I'll figure something out, but I have to head out. Class starts soon. Thanks for meeting me."

"Always."

I felt my brother's eyes on my back as I wove through the tables to the door. I stopped to guzzle the rest of my drink before tossing the cup and leaving. I needed all the caffeine I could get. I wasn't sleeping well. Every time I closed my eyes, I remembered the way Luke's body had folded when he'd fallen back, his head landing on that damn step with a deafening thud. His arm had flopped, coming up slightly as if he were reaching for life, only to fall limply back at his side.

As I walked down the sidewalk, each step felt weighted with more problems than I was sure I could manage. I couldn't help but realize that my issue with the art professor wasn't even the biggest one I had to worry about.

CHAPTER FIVE

WINTER

Mornings were difficult, and that one was no exception—what I wouldn't give to wake up in Brooke and James's house. She knew me well and would make coffee before my horrid alarm went off, hoping to lure me from sleep first with the heavenly scent wafting under my door from the kitchen. The decadent aroma of roasted beans and whatever gourmet breakfast she made had always altered my grouchy morning self into something halfway human.

I had to make adjustments. The dorm and being away at college was another reality I had to get used to. I should have been a pro by then. And to say I felt optimistic about the change in environment was a gross misconception. So far, the shrill beep of my phone's alarm only made me wake with a groan. Good thing Piper was already out of the room and probably in some ridiculously early class.

After a half-awake shower and managing to pull on clothes for my first day, I packed my oversized messenger bag with everything I might need for class. I had twenty minutes to spare before the first one, which would work well for getting breakfast. My keys were on the desk, and I grabbed them just as a brisk knock sounded on the door.

I set my bag down, flipped the lock, and opened the door. A fortyish, petite redhead with bright-green eyes stood there. "Brooke."

"Morning, sunshine." She held out a to-go cup.

My greedy hand grasped it and brought it straight to my lips. The first sip sang through my body, kick-starting my brain enough that I stepped aside for her to enter. "What are you doing here?" That was when I noticed the tiny lines bracketing her mouth and etched between her brows. "That sounded rude. I didn't mean it like that."

A small smile curved her lips, and she visibly softened. "I know you didn't."

"What is it then?" I grinned. "Did you miss me?" Part of me tensed to hear her response. And though she always made sure I felt welcomed, wanted, and loved, the little girl in me braced for rejection. The truth was that I missed the hell out of her and the family I'd been included in.

"Of course, we miss you. With you and Jaxon at college, it's lonely at home." She squeezed my arm before sitting at my desk and glancing at the pink explosion opposite my bed. "How's it going with the roommate?"

I shrugged. "Good. I know her from when I went to elementary school in Santa Monica. We used to be friends, and we even went to an off-campus coffee place yesterday, where I can see myself establishing residency for homework."

"The Spot." Brooke laughed. "It was around back in the day when James and I went to college here. It's where we met."

"I didn't know that." The smokin' hot athlete came to mind. *Wouldn't it be funny if something developed between us and I could tell Brooke where I met him?* I sat on my bed rather than hover awkwardly.

"I'm sure it looks different inside, but it was where James

and I spent a good portion of our Sundays getting work done, as opposed to the library."

I glanced at the time.

"Oh." Brooke dug around in her oversized purse. "I brought you a piece of coffee cake too."

My shoulders eased when she produced the cinnamon streusel. I popped the top off the container and dug in with the fork she gave me. When the sugar hit my tongue, I moaned with happiness, my eyes drifting shut briefly. I could almost imagine being back in her kitchen.

When I opened my eyes, it was to the sight of her pinched expression, and I tensed. *No.* She may have come because she missed me, but there was another reason behind the early-morning visit. Dread weighed heavily on my shoulders. "Just tell me."

She deflated. "I didn't want to do this on your first day, but it's important." After digging around in her purse, she produced two letters. One with California State Penitentiary stamped in the upper-left-hand corner and the other from the parole board. Both were addressed to me.

I didn't want to take them from her. I knew the day was coming, but I'd preferred to stick my head in the sand until I couldn't any longer. It looked like that day had come. The food I'd wolfed down sat like lead in my stomach, and I pushed the container away. "I don't want to read them."

Brooke leaned forward and covered my hand with hers. "I think you should open the parole one at the very least."

I turned my head away but kept my hand in hers. I hated my mom. The few good moments with her were so few and far between. But nothing good I remembered outweighed what she'd done countless times to my sister and me. *Especially my sister.*

"You know James and I think of you as our daughter. And even though your mom wouldn't grant us adoption rights—"

"Which is bullshit. She shouldn't be able to retain any rights."

"Well, it doesn't matter. In our hearts, you are our daughter. And I know Jaxon feels the same about you being his sister."

I sucked in a shaky breath as a rogue tear fell. "Why won't she just go away?" The heated words were filled with venom.

"Oh, Winter." Brooke got up and pulled me into her arms.

I felt sheltered. Safe. In that moment, anyway. But the letter's presence still lingered. She was right. I needed to know. I couldn't allow to be blindsided by anything regarding my mom. A sliver of loneliness seeped back when she released me, and I straightened my spine against it.

"I'm here for you, always. You know that, right?" Brooke hooked two fingers under my chin and tilted my head so our eyes met. Hers were bright, holding back her unshed tears.

I cleared my throat so I could speak past the lump that had lodged there. "I do."

My hand shook as I picked up the offensive letter and slid my finger under the envelope flap, tugging against the seam until it ripped. I took another deep breath and withdrew the white piece of paper, unfolding it a moment later. There wasn't much to it, and I skimmed it before rereading it, my heart beating furiously against my chest.

"She has a hearing for early release, and I'm invited to speak on her behalf." A buzzing noise filled my ears. I dropped the letter and backed away from it. "She has two more years. Why would they release her early?" My shrill voice cut through the odd buzzing, and I jerked my gaze to Brooke.

Her lips moved, but I couldn't hear her. I grabbed onto her arms, and she did to mine. Seconds passed where I couldn't catch my breath. Then the buzzing receded, and Brooke's voice broke through. Tremors shook my body, and she pried her arms from my too-tight grip, sat on the bed, and pulled me into her embrace, rocking me back and forth.

Eventually, the shock ebbed, but I didn't move away. I

couldn't live without her whispered mantra that everything would be okay or the comfort she offered me. Not yet. I didn't care that I was eighteen or that my reaction seemed childish. That letter shook my world in the worst way.

"Why now?"

"When your mom was sentenced to ten years, the judge said she had to serve eighty percent of it before being eligible for parole. She's at that milestone."

I closed my eyes, wishing it away. It was childish. I knew that.

"I talked to our lawyer." Brooke ran a hand down my hair. "And he said that this is her first hearing. She'll get one every six months until she's either granted parole or has served all ten years."

"It's not long enough." Pure hatred for that woman filled me. "It'll never be long enough."

Brooke said nothing, just continued to hold me until I was ready to let go.

"Do you want to come home? You don't have to start this semester. You can defer until next year."

That wouldn't solve anything. "No. But thank you."

"Oh, Winter. You can always come home."

"I know." And I did.

The Childress family had made that abundantly clear throughout my years with them. When I'd acted out and shoved them away that first year, testing them to do their worst, they never did. Even Jaxon stayed by my side. They might not be blood, but what they'd given me was better. I couldn't let them down. I was made of much stronger stuff. I had to be to survive what I had.

"Do you want to go shopping today? Or maybe walk around the art museum then get lunch?"

I pulled back, and her arms fell away. "Thank you. As much as I want to ditch and hang out with you, I need to get to class."

She cupped the side of my face. "Are you okay? I hate leaving you like this."

"I will be. Promise."

She gave me a slight nod. "If you change your mind, I can be in the car and pick you up in thirty minutes. I'm not doing anything today."

I knew her well enough that she would make sure she was available for me all day, just in case.

We talked for another ten minutes until I had to splash some water on my face then go to class. I promised I would call her later in the afternoon and tell her about my first day. She said she would pop in on Jaxon before she left. Her eyes had sparkled at the thought of surprising her son.

I grinned because he was probably still sleeping. He wasn't a morning person either. It was too bad we didn't have classes together, but I'd taken what I could.

I'd gotten into art because of Jaxon. When we were little, he'd been the one always drawing or painting, and he would drag me outside to do it with him. I'd missed Summer so severely that I hadn't fought him. We had both been alone, neither of us having a sibling. So we'd formed a bond. I wasn't half bad at drawing and would always owe him for that. It gave me a sense of peace most of the time.

The walk to Professor Elian's class felt as if I were in a bubble. I got there, but I didn't remember how. When I found an empty seat seconds before class started, I pulled out my sketchbook and charcoal pencils. I'd been so excited to take the class, but I could only pay partial attention as she reviewed the project we would work on for the next two weeks.

Since I was toward the back of the class, I let my hand fly across the paper, sketching the same portrait I had since I was twelve. I knew why the faceless man had appeared ominously in charcoal—I could feel Mom breathing down my neck with her possible early release. No matter how hard I tried to bury the past, there was no escape. It was coming for me.

After stopping at the cafeteria, I followed the walkway to Jaxon's dorm. Since he had started at Thane the first semester, I'd visited before with Brooke and James and had helped him move in. He was on the fourth floor. That had been a pain to move him into. My room was on the third and hadn't been a piece of cake with the stairs either. It wouldn't have been so difficult if only the elevator had been unlocked. And if I'd told my foster brother or let Brooke and James help me like they'd wanted to.

Neither one of us had classes for the rest of the day, and I'd brought a peace offering—art supplies. Whenever we got the chance, we tried to spend time working together on whatever project we had. I trudged up the stairs, securing my messenger bag over my shoulder a little better.

His dorm was busier, and I passed several students on the stairs. My legs burned by the time I got to his floor. Gah, I needed to get back into running. That was ridiculous. I went down one hallway, rounded another, and stopped in front of his door. I rapped my knuckles on it then waited. It didn't take long.

Jax yanked open the door, filling it with his linebacker-ish build. It cracked me up that such a big guy wasn't on the football team. He played sports for fun, but his real passion was art. His parents were cool about it, encouraging him in whatever made him happy. It had been such a foreign concept when I'd first joined their household.

A frown marred his face, and he shoved a clump of auburn hair off his forehead. He looked like he'd come straight from the studio, in basketball shorts and a gray shirt splattered with paint. It was his usual outfit.

"Huh, finally decided to let me know you're alive and actually a student here?"

Yep, he was still mad. "I'm sorry. I just needed to deal with it on my own."

"That's bullshit, and you know it."

It was, but I was just as stubborn as he was. "Whatever." I pulled the strap of my bag so it swung forward. "Do you have time to sketch? Maybe we could go outside."

He crossed his arms, not budging.

"I brought sandwiches."

That should do it. He was always hungry, and the fridge at the Childress's house was jam-packed at all times. I could recall standing in front of it in shock the first time I'd opened it. When he looked to the ceiling then back again, I knew I had him, especially since the corner of his mouth twitched up just a little.

"So...?"

"Yeah, we can do that. But I'm not done being mad at you." He stepped back so I could come in.

"Yes, you are." I elbowed him in the side. He was a big softie. "I'm sorry I didn't call you as soon as I got here and have you help me. I was just... I don't know. In a mood."

"When aren't you?"

I grinned, happy we were back to teasing each other. I glanced around while he grabbed a blue backpack and added a few things from his desk. A framed picture held a collage of his parents and us from the summer vacation we'd taken the first year after I'd moved in with them. I'd never taken a vacation before that, and I'd loved every second of it with my new family. The rest of the room was typical Jaxon. The bed was made. No clothes littered the floor, and he even had an illegal candle on his desk. We were only allowed to have battery ones. A small fridge and band posters were mixed in with some of his artwork.

"How did you manage not to have a roommate?" I was kind of jealous.

"I asked if you wanted to room with me."

I snorted. "And cramp your style? I'm not that mean. But also, the school wouldn't have allowed it."

"Funny, right? I'm the least of their concerns with a girl, yet they roomed me with a guy." He winked. "You have to meet Max."

"Who wasn't your roommate. I bet you got a straight guy, so, what you're hinting at doesn't count."

He grinned. "True that."

"I look forward to meeting Max, though. Maybe we can get together on one of the weekends and, I don't know, go bowling or something?"

It was one of the activities we did as a family at least twice a week. I'd gotten addicted to it. Mostly because Jaxon and I did everything we could to make the other mess up when it was our turn. I'd never thought having a brother could be so much fun. It helped with how much I missed Summer, which he probably knew. I was fortunate.

"I'll talk to Max. Oh, and Winter…" He turned and looked at me with pure joy in his hazel eyes. "You're gonna love him as much as I do."

Everything in me softened and warmed. "If he's good to you and makes you happy, I will."

After he zipped his bag and slung it over his shoulder, we headed out. Most of the people we passed on his floor called a greeting to him, which he returned. I was used to it. That was how it had been in high school too. He was charismatic, steady, and kind. People gravitated toward him.

We went outside, walked a little, and found a great spot under a palm tree in the west courtyard, where it wasn't overly busy. Jaxon pulled out a woven blanket he'd stuffed into his bag and spread it on the ground. I was grateful. Bugs and I didn't get along.

I pulled out my sketchbook and charcoal pencils then paused. "Hey, do you have Professor Elian?"

"Nope." Jaxon opened his large colored case I envied. It had over a hundred pencils in all shades. "I have Professor Potts. Why?"

"She's kind of… distracted." I couldn't think of any other word that would describe the weird vibe I got from her.

"Potts is strict. Artists are spacey, which you should know. Maybe that's why?"

I smacked him on the shoulder with my sketchpad. "Hey, speak for yourself. I'm only a wannabe artist compared to you." I snagged one of his purple pencils and rolled it between my fingers before reluctantly returning it.

"I wouldn't worry about your teacher. If you don't like her, drop the class."

"Um, no. I couldn't get into any others since I signed up late." It was already second semester. "I'll deal and try your class next year."

He slid over a small tin of colored pencils.

"What's this?"

"It's a welcome-to-Thane gift." Then he pulled out a couple of small paintbrushes, a bottled water, and a small dish. "They're watercolor pencils. After you finish your drawing, you can turn it into a watercolor picture. I thought you might like them."

"I love them." I tore the cellophane off and opened them. I would work on that this afternoon. Screw sticking to charcoal pencils. I leaned over and wrapped my arms around Jaxon. "Thank you."

"You're welcome." He squeezed me back before letting go. "I'm glad you decided to come to Thane. You'll love it here."

That remained to be seen, but I kept my skepticism to

myself. "Oh! I forgot." I pulled out the sandwiches and handed him one.

Jaxon groaned when he opened the extra-meat-and-cheese sub with bacon I'd gotten him. "Okay, you're forgiven."

"The way to your heart is definitely through your stomach." I giggled. "Does Max know that yet?"

"Probably," he said around a mouthful. "How's the new roommate?"

"You'll never believe it." I filled him in on how Piper had been one of my sister's friends, a year older than me, and that I'd also been on friendly terms with her because of Summer. "I recognized her right away. It was so weird."

"Are you okay living with her?" Concern darkened his eyes, and he watched me closely.

"Yeah." I shrugged. "I don't have a problem with Piper. And having a roommate, putting myself out there, and getting to know people is sort of the reason I transferred here. Well, that and to dig into my past a little."

His eyebrows rose, and he lowered what remained of his food. "So, you're going through with that? Have you read the letters yet?"

My stomach clenched painfully. "No." I looked away, studying the students and faculty that walked past. "I still can't bring myself to read them." *What could my mom say after what she'd done to us?*

Jaxon situated himself so his back rested against the tree we sat under, mirroring my pose. Our shoulders brushed against each other's as he drew up his knees and balanced his sketch-book, creating an easel of sorts. I did the same. It was how we worked sometimes when we went outside back home.

"I'm here for you, Winter. Don't forget that."

I rested my head on his shoulder for a second. "Yeah, I know. Thanks."

"Brooke stopped by early this morning. She said she planned

to see you right after." Maybe I should've taken him up on rooming together, or incognito because Thane wouldn't agree to it. "Hey, you never said how you got a private room."

"My roommate transferred. He was from Colorado and missed his family. He's going to Colorado State instead."

"But you didn't get another one?"

"I asked Mom and Dad if we could swing the extra cost for a single. I wanted more space to paint and draw in my room rather than always having to go to the studio."

"Um, we're working outside. What's the big deal?"

"You're well aware that I wake up sometimes in the middle of the night and want to paint, and if I don't, I can't fall back asleep."

"Oh, right. I forgot about that."

It hadn't affected me because his parents had set up an extra room at home as a studio for Jaxon. I'd stumbled across him one night when I'd had a nightmare.

We fell into silence, the only sound between us the scratch of the pencils against the paper. I'd chosen to draw a section of the building across from us. The architecture was intricate and drew the eye. I altered it slightly so it was even more old-world looking. As it took shape, I toyed with putting someone in one of the windows. I might still do that.

"Do you still draw him?"

I started then scowled at Jaxon. He was lucky I'd paused, or I would have dug the pencil into the paper. "Yes."

No reason to clarify. The talk about Jax painting at night had triggered the memory of me coming across him for both of us. A few times, I'd covered the walls in the studio room with charcoal renderings of what I saw in my dreams. Before he could tell Brooke and James, I'd destroyed the evidence. I had been terrified that it would somehow make them want me to leave or that social services would swoop in and take me away, labeling me a risk. It was ridiculous, but I couldn't help it. I was very protective of the family I'd been included in and tried to hide the darker side of myself, the one that seemed to awaken in my dreams.

"They have counselors here. No one has to know if you see someone." Worry coated his words. "It might help."

"Maybe." My pencil hovered over the page. "I'll think about it."

I knew it bothered Jaxon. He'd witnessed so many things I'd drawn, and not just the faceless man but of my life with my sister. I always shredded the drawings after I created them. It was cathartic to get some of what I'd lived through out of my head then destroy it.

It'd become a regular thing for a while, the two of us awake at odd hours during the night, working away together in the studio, in silence.

"Jaxon, I promise I'll tell you if I'm struggling. But right now," I pleaded with him, "I just want to be normal, to put myself out there and make some friends."

I hadn't even tried it while we were in high school. I was friends with the people he was closest to because I'd tagged along. Or Jaxon had made me. But college was my time. I'd promised myself and Brooke that among other things. I didn't want to think about the rest right then. It was enough that I wanted to try.

"Have some faith in me."

I needed all I could get, and my brother was the best person around to have on my side. I nudged him. "Hey, I wanted to hang with you and find out about Max. We're getting too deep here for my first week at Thane. Spill. Tell me everything."

Jaxon laughed, and the sound was so carefree and happy that it seeped into the cracks in my soul. I needed that, and I would soak up every minute I could with him, leaving the scary stuff for another day.

CHAPTER SIX

SHANE

I'm not the same person I was in fifth grade. I'm Shane fucking Bennett, star football player and NFL draft contender. I looped that repeatedly, working hard to dispel the replay of nightmares —*of memories*—I'd been caught in last night. The sense of helplessness and fear about going to school and what the girl I'd had the biggest crush on would do to me next.

No more. It was payback time.

I hardened myself against the image of her today, as opposed to when we were kids. She looked pretty well-adjusted, confident and beautiful with all that amazing strawberry-blond hair that I wanted to wrap around my fist or see fanned across my pillow. I knew from experience she didn't have the heart to feel what I did, but I could certainly make sure she became acquainted with the despair and humiliation I had experienced at my lowest. I would find a way to make her pay.

My mind was too foggy from back-to-back classes and lack of sleep to figure out a plan yet, but I would. It was only a matter of time because the kid inside me deserved the chance to get back at her.

Muted sound traveled under the closed door from my teammates moving around in the football house. In my room, it was quiet enough. I used to share the space with Phoenix before he moved out and into married housing with Aspen for the current semester. I was still getting used to that, as I imagined they were too.

My stomach rumbled. I needed food. I shoved my wallet into my back pocket and headed out to Dillon's Diner, where Joe, my dad, wanted to meet.

Mixed feelings plagued me on the ride there, and I sat in my Range Rover for a few minutes after parking. Phoenix and Mom were wary of the man who had abandoned us when she was pregnant with us. The reasons he'd listed when he'd reached out at the beginning of my first semester at Thane had seemed valid, but I'd known Phoenix would be a tough sell, so I had waited to share the news. The timing had sucked, and I would always regret what had happened when I'd brought my brother to the hotel where Joe—our dad—was staying.

I was the only one who would talk to Joe. The others weren't ready or willing to let him into any part of their lives. But I'd been given many second chances in my life, and the jury was still out on which would go well. Tracey, my former girlfriend, had tried to get back together with me after dumping me so brutally. I'd entertained the possibility and hooked up with her several times, but the betrayal had cut too deep.

As for the opportunity that had fallen into my lap when Phoenix and I had gone for coffee, that was just the beginning. And I was eager to get some revenge on Winter. It felt like the one thing in my damned life that I had any control over.

Joe's second chance was underway, and I hoped with every-thing in me that we could build a relationship. I left my car and entered the diner, spotting Joe quickly—it was still difficult to think of him as my father.

I slid into the booth with two menus already on the table. The waitress came over immediately, and we both placed our orders since I knew what I wanted from eating there often enough. When she left, I studied Joe like I had every time I'd met him. The similarities between him and Phoenix were uncanny. We were fraternal twins. I looked more like Mom than I did Joe. It bothered my brother that he and Joe resembled each other, and I could understand that, even if I hoped we could put the past behind us and become the family we never had been.

"No Phoenix?"

I shook my head. Joe asked whenever we met, and I always confirmed the obvious. My brother wasn't interested in a relationship. He'd told me Joe couldn't be trusted despite the evidence our dad had presented against our mom's dad, Grandad, and his involvement in our dad's absence from our lives. I didn't fully understand Phoenix's reservations. Joe had shown us the absurdly large and uncashed check Grandad had bribed him with to stay away from Mom.

He studied me for a moment, and it felt like ants crawling all over me with how stressed I was. Things were escalating. I couldn't sleep without reliving my fist hitting Luke, then him falling, his head cracking open on the step. The blood. The yellow fluid—spinal fluid. The last rasp of breath as it left his mouth then nothing. It played on repeat when I wasn't busy. The guilt and horror ate at me, and I couldn't talk to my brother about it. He had Aspen and the baby to worry about. School. Football. His plate was full. I refused to tip it over.

"It'll work out." Joe's voice pulled me from my thoughts.

"What will?"

"The legal stuff you've got going on." His dark-silver eyes hardened. "Remember I told you about the legal trouble I got into as a kid?"

"Yeah. You grew up in the foster system and something about killing someone."

"I never wanted to share this with you boys, but maybe you need to hear it. I was thirteen, when someone attacked the house where a bunch of us foster kids were living. The family got more money that way. But one of the kids, he was no good. He went after us, and I'd had enough. It wasn't just for me. I was protecting another kid."

I remembered some of the story, not the details because he hadn't given those. "You were sentenced for murder."

"I was underage. Thirteen. And yes, I'd stabbed the kid enough times that he bled out. I did time in juvie and later changed my name. I got through it. You will too. Survival is in your blood."

I didn't like the smile that curved his lips like he was proud. *Of murder?* It didn't sit right with me. But maybe that wasn't it. I wasn't sleeping, so I was probably reading things wrong. He was trying to connect, to offer support and advice.

"I'm an adult. Things work differently when you're not a juvenile."

"People with money rule. And you've got your grandad on your side."

I hoped like hell he was right. "I don't think it'll be enough."

"Shane." Joe's hands curled into fists on top of the table. "There's no way I'll let you go to jail. And if your grandfather won't help with his family ties, then I will. I know the same people."

"What are you talking about? What people?"

"You don't know?" Mocking laughter fell from his mouth. "Your grandfather is a third cousin to the Bennett crime family."

I shook my head, speechless. *Mafia?* "No. I don't believe you."

He shrugged. "It doesn't matter. What does is if things go south, they own judges. I promise you won't go to jail."

Our drinks arrived, and I was glad for the distraction, needing to process everything he'd just laid on me. Until Joe pulled out a bound packet and slid it across the table to me.

"What's this?" Wrenshall & Sons Construction was printed on the cover.

He tapped it just beneath the name. "It's a business plan and contract. I want to go into business with you boys—flipping houses."

I could barely process his words. *Why?* It didn't make sense. "What about football? How would you have time for something like that?"

Joe was on Chicago's team, but from the little I'd paid attention to his career, I did know he rarely, if ever, left the bench.

His eyes, more gray than silver, hardened, and lines bracketed his mouth. "They didn't renew my contract. And after a series of bad investments, I really need something like this. It's a fresh start, a foolproof one, and a way to reconnect, father and sons."

"That sucks." I wasn't surprised he'd been dropped, but when football was a person's life, getting let go was devastating, nonetheless. And football had seemed to be everything to him after he'd walked away from us. "So." I shifted uncomfortably then glanced at the softbound bundle of papers, *Wrenshall & Sons* glaring at me in bold font. "You have experience in flipping homes?"

We fell silent as the waitress brought our burgers. I took a big bite while I waited for his response.

He leaned back in his seat, an arm flung along the back of the green vinyl bench. "Your mom didn't tell you?"

An uncomfortable heaviness settled between us as tension built between my shoulder blades. In one look, I telegraphed that he'd better watch his step in any conversations regarding my mom. He seemed to pick up on it as a slow grin replaced the previous hard slash of his mouth.

"Construction was how I put myself through college." He picked up a fry and pointed it at me. "I didn't have a crazy scholarship like your brother, or even yours."

How does he know about that? I finished off my burger as he took his first bite.

"Hasn't your agent reached out to other teams?" I started on my fries.

"I decided that wasn't in the cards. Now that we're in contact, I thought it would be best to make up for lost time. Going into business together would give us that." He slid the packet closer to me. "We would buy a house on the cheap, fix it up, and sell it for ten times our original investment."

I wasn't unfamiliar with HGTV, as Mom loved to watch stuff on it. I knew about the concept of flipping houses, and he made it sound so easy, but things rarely were. "Phoenix and I don't have that kind of time. We both have school and football. I'm sure you remember how hard that was without adding in a start-up." Not to mention the hours I had to work for Grandad until he felt I'd learned my lesson and eased some of the lawyer's fee.

It wasn't a bad idea, and I would need a backup plan since I'd killed someone and was still on shaky ground with what additional fallout could come of it. But there had to be a catch. And the fact that I still didn't know what I wanted to do for a backup plan, aside from business and work for Grandad, was what kept me in my seat with a reticently open mind to the project.

Joe flipped the book open a few pages to where the contract disclosed the start-up costs. "I know your grandad set up trusts for you boys"—he tapped beneath the excessive amount—"so this shouldn't be an issue. We each go in equally, and we buy our first house. I'll have the controlling share, but that's because I'll also be the general manager on the projects, as you're focused elsewhere until school is finished."

"I don't have the kind of money to put in to be partners."

"You have the trust." He folded his arms on the table, the plate of food in front of him forgotten. "And I have my share, but I gotta get things going before my debts are called due."

That didn't sound good. He must be more overextended than he'd let on.

"I don't have access to the trust. My mom and Grandad have control of that, and it won't be mine for several more years." We'd only recently become aware of that fact, and it would be nice if Grandad could release it early instead of wanting us to "build character."

Joe smirked. "You can borrow against it."

How does Joe know about the trust? Phoenix and I'd only found out recently. And the bank was watching it like a hawk for Grandad. *So could I borrow against it?* Probably not.

Joe flagged down the waitress. After she gave him the bill, he dropped some cash on the table to cover it and waved to me.

"Come on. I want to show you the first house we'll buy."

We left, and I climbed into his old but new-to-him Bronco. *And why didn't he just buy a new car?* He had all that NFL money, even if he had been picked last as Mr. Irrelevant all those years ago. It bothered me enough to ask as he backed out of the parking lot and pointed us away from the college.

"This is a work truck. I didn't see the point of wasting hard-earned money on something that will only get scratched up from hauling materials."

Makes sense. "How far is the house?" When I returned, I had a paper to write, and if I had time, I wanted to hit the gym again.

"Forty-five minutes away, give or take."

Fuck. That wouldn't be even remotely possible to manage. I clenched my teeth almost the entire drive. And when we got there, he threw the SUV in park and hopped out. I reluctantly followed, meeting him in front of the car.

He clapped my shoulder and dragged me closer, excitedly waving his other arm around. "Just look at the potential here."

I looked, but what I saw was a boarded-up, slant-roofed house. "It's rough." And that was only the outside. I wanted no part of going in and seeing the amount of "potential" he'd mentioned.

"It's in an up-and-coming neighborhood, and the housing

market is hot now. We need to hurry before someone else snaps up this gem."

I tuned him out, losing interest faster than words spewed from his mouth. It wasn't my thing, and the thought of taking on anything else seemed ridiculous. He had enthusiasm for the project and the company that he wanted to build with me and my brother. Maybe even enough for the both of us. But I wasn't on board yet, and he could tell from my expression.

The ride back was a hard sell, and my mind spun with how much he pushed the issue.

"I need your deposit and Phoenix's soon so we don't lose the house."

I found that hard to believe but kept my mouth shut and eyes forward, willing the diner to appear much earlier than it would. I wouldn't touch on the topic of my brother. "The distance to school is too great. I can't manage that with all my other commitments."

"You don't need to worry about that because I'll manage the work. I have a contractor lined up. I just need the thirty grand to buy it and maybe another twenty to put in."

"I don't have that kind of bank."

Joe glanced at me, his brows raised, before returning to the road. "Your car is worth a hell of a lot more than that, and you could always get the money from your grandfather. He's loaded."

No way would Grandad lend me that kind of money, especially to work with Joe Wrenshall.

"If I have to get the money from someone else, I will. I just thought this would be something we could do together, since I didn't get to do things with you guys before."

My head throbbed. "I don't know."

"Don't mention this deal to anyone just yet."

Right, who would I mention it to? Phoenix didn't trust him, and Grandad would run him out of the state if he could. Joe turned right, and I almost sighed in relief. We were about five blocks from the diner.

"I doubt Phoenix would want to be in on this."

"We can bring him in after we have a return to show him. And of course, in addition to the initial investment of fifty grand, you will get half the profit to show your brother."

It would give me the money to pay back Grandad. And if things went south and the NFL wouldn't touch me because of Luke, or if they found out about the underground fights, it would be an option for my future.

"I'll try to get you the money." I regretted it as the words left my mouth. I really should talk to Grandad about it.

Joe's excitement was almost infectious. Not enough to make the dread weighing me down go away, but his enthusiasm made me hope it could bridge the gap between the rest of my family and him. Maybe we could finally be a family.

When I got to the Range Rover Uncle Lucas had bought me and that I loved, I couldn't help but think about what a weird day it had been. Fuck the paper I should be working on. When I got back to the football house, the idea of throwing a party took root. Maybe then I could get drunk enough to sleep through the night. I would figure out how to get Joe the money in the morning.

CHAPTER SEVEN

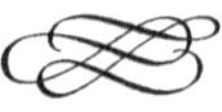

WINTER

Music pulsed through the darkness, drawing me closer to the party at the football house Piper had texted me about. I'd never been to a college party and was mildly annoyed she hadn't waited for me. But she'd gone with some of her friends and had extended the invite, which I guessed I was grateful for.

I smoothed my hand down my hair, partially wishing that I'd done something more with it than run a brush through the long strands. But I wasn't one of those girls with perfect hair, makeup, or clothes. I wasn't even that experienced with boys—like hardly at all. Sure, I'd been on a handful of dates. But they'd never gone anywhere because I didn't want to be away from the Childresses that often or let anyone else get close.

I had the Childress family, and the last thing I needed was to become my mom. Which meant guys and dating were a very low priority. College had changed the game all over again. Even though Jaxon was here, I felt alone. The rules were different—which was why I'd even entertained going to the party.

My dorm was only a few blocks from the football house. It

made sense to walk. If I wanted to drink, I wouldn't need to call a ride, though more than one drink was unlikely.

Another wave of insecurity swept over me. Thanks to Mom, I never let anyone get close—the Childress family being the only exception and, to an extent, Piper when she was friends with my sister. That said, I didn't know how to dress for the party. I wore faded jeans and a dark-blue, long-sleeved T-shirt and called it good.

Old-fashioned lantern-like lights dotted the side of the pathways, giving the campus a prestigious and academic flair. The farther from the dorms, the closer I got to the party. The music grew louder, a thumping bass that I adjusted my footfalls to match the closer I got. I couldn't have missed it if I'd tried and laughed under my breath. The house was a massive three-story building with windows blazing and people milling about. Those blow-up kid pools were scattered on the grass, some full of beer, others of people—insane people. It was winter, even though it was a relatively mild California night. *Still...*

Piper had said she was on the front lawn when she messaged me, and I scanned the growing crowd for her blond head. I spotted her next to one of the kiddie pools and headed over.

She must have seen me from the corner of her eye because she turned as I approached. "You made it!" Her eyes were dilated, and her smile wide.

"Yeah." I visually swept the lawn and house, noting that some of the girls were dressed similarly to me. Most showed way more skin. "This place is crazy."

"Brian, get my friend a drink."

The linebacker-sized guy standing with two others bent, fished a White Claw from the ice, and handed it to me.

"Thanks." I took the drink and popped it open but didn't take a sip. It was a prop only.

Piper's hand landed on my arm, and she steered me to another area on the lawn. "Before I texted you, I didn't think I would actually come here." She pursed her lips then gave the football house the finger. "But screw 'em. I'm a different person this year."

"Okay." I had no idea what that was all about. "Did you date someone who lives here?"

She snorted, leaning heavily against my side. "Nooooo, but I sure as shit wanted to. I thought Cole and I were something in high school." Her arm flailed around her body as she talked. "Screw him. Turns out we were nothing. And now, she's got him."

"Who's got him?"

"Another girl. Who cares? I'm over him. This year is about me."

I grinned. She was hilarious when drunk. "You go, girl. Who needs a guy? That's what vibrators are for."

Her head tilted to the side, and she took me in again. "Winter, I was wrong about you. I think we're gonna be great friends."

My teeth sank into my bottom lip. Partly so I wouldn't laugh in her face. She was entertaining. And I could use a friend. "Sounds like a plan, Pipes."

"Let's go to the Spot tomorrow."

"Okay. I'm game." It was weird, though. She said that like she wasn't hanging with me here. *Maybe I misunderstood her earlier text?*

"Piper!" some girl about five feet away from us hollered.

A giggle spilled from Piper's ruby lips. "That's Tracey." She extracted her hand from my arm and took a hesitant step toward the other girl. "Come on."

She tugged at my arm to drag me over, but something held me back. "I'm going to wander around a bit. I'll catch you later."

"Sure. I'll see you in a bit. Or..." She giggled. "Back in the room if you're looking to score some action here."

I snorted. Maybe that was her plan, to get some action,

because the guys watched as she stumbled across the lawn toward her BFF. I wasn't sure if she would end up back at her friend's place or with one of those guys.

With a cursory glance, I held onto my drink and didn't see anyone else I knew, which was zero people, really, aside from Jax. But maybe I could find the hot guy from the Spot. Something told me he would be there. I rolled my eyes at myself. The thought wasn't as profound as it had seemed at first. It was easy to assume because of all the similarly built guys there.

Head high, I wove through partiers until I made it to the stairs that would take me to the porch and wide-open door to the house. I crossed the threshold and took a beat to brace myself against the sheer volume of music flooding the space. A crush of people stood inside, and I edged my way along the outer wall.

I pushed out another breath. My third since Piper had traipsed off to join her friend. My nerves were getting the best of me. They weren't about the party, not really. It was him. I could feel him somewhere in there. Weirdest thing ever, but every inch of me was hyperaware of his larger-than-life presence, and I swore he was inside the huge house because that was where I felt most drawn.

And the weirdest thing, I didn't even know his name. But every journey started with a single step, and that was mine—to take back my life. Being there was surreal. It wasn't exactly where I grew up, but it was close enough and around people from the same school I'd attended years ago. Brooke and I had discussed my attending Thane and conquering old ghosts many times.

Another visual sweep of drunk partygoers, and I suppressed my dislike for everything it encompassed. I wasn't a partier. But that didn't matter. I was back, and it was time to take full control of my life.

I eased around two girls, and that was when I saw him

standing in a doorway, hands holding onto the frame over his head, muscles bulging. My mouth watered at the picture he presented. I never looked twice at the big, brawny types. They hadn't been my jam before, but I couldn't take my eyes off him.

Every visible inch of him drew me in, but I held my stance. *Would he see me, remember me?* I didn't flirt or chase after anyone, so the whole thing was foreign territory. *I... I just want something for me that isn't in my plan. Or maybe this is?* Taking back my life could entail letting someone else in, even a little bit.

The fine hair on the back of my neck rose as his gaze locked on mine. He said something to the brunette with her hair slicked back into a high ponytail then broke off their conversation as he walked toward me. The crowd parted for him.

It was loud, and I had no idea how we would converse, but I wanted to. A beer bottle dangled from his fingers. A slight grin curved his lips, and his eyes smoldered. He glanced pointedly at the drink I held, and I shook my head. I didn't need another. I hadn't even drunk a sip yet. When he reached me, he settled his large hand on the small of my back. The tiniest bit of pressure had me moving in the direction he wanted me to go—toward the rear door.

He pushed open the screen, and we walked out onto a deck. I glanced at him out of the corner of my eye, wondering how I could tactfully ask his name. Nothing clever came to mind, and when we stopped in a dimly lit corner of the yard, a reasonable distance from the deck, I took the standard route.

"I'm Winter."

His hand fell away, and we faced one another as he took a long pull from his beer. Dark-blue eyes held mine, his expression giving nothing away. "I know who you are."

"Oh?" I scanned his face, trying to find something familiar. I drew a blank, and when a slow, wicked grin curved his kissable lips, I stopped trying to place him.

"I make sure to know all the beautiful women."

I shifted from foot to foot, heat climbing up my neck and settling in my cheeks. He was a total player. "Maybe this was a mistake."

Strong, warm fingers loosely encircled my wrist, and I froze at how the slightest contact sent bolts of electricity surging through my body.

"Don't go. I want to get to know you."

I tilted my head. I couldn't figure him out. If nothing else, I owed it to myself to see where our crazy chemistry would lead, if only because I'd never felt anything like it before, and I was more than a little curious. "Do you live here?" I flicked my gaze over his shoulder at the brightly lit house looming behind us.

"Yeah. I'm on the football team." He released me, his gaze bouncing over my face, searching. "You don't remember who I am?"

I gave a slight shake of my head.

"We went to elementary school together."

That explained why I had no idea who he was, not really. I only remembered Piper because Summer was best friends with her. Those years, especially the last one, had been shitty. Mom was doing a lot of drugs. Men were in and out of the house, and my grandparents wanted nothing to do with us. The reference to that time shook me, and I didn't want to admit I had no clue who he was. "Oh, right. It's great to see you again."

He didn't give anything away. Not even his name. Frustration clawed at me, but not enough for me to ask. Something held me back. Maybe it was how his features began to change. His eyes narrowed, and his mouth formed a tight line. A girl shrieked, and I glanced toward the sound. Some guy chased her around the yard. Both were laughing. He caught her and swung her around, then over his shoulder, before bounding up the porch steps and into the house.

When I swiveled back to the nameless blue-eyed man, I thought I might be going crazy. *Did I imagine how hard he looked a moment ago?* I gave myself a mental shake because his face was back to normal as he smiled at me, and something about the intensity in his eyes made me want to take a risk, stay, and get to know him a little.

"How do you like playing for the team?"

"It's everything I'd hoped it would be, aside from the injury I had at the beginning of the season. That cost me a few games. But next year will be even better. How about you? Are you in any sports? Or are you here strictly for academics?"

"Academics. Art mainly. I've never gotten into sports." That would have burned precious calories when I was young. And in Brooke and James's care, it never occurred to me to try.

"And you're a transfer? Where did you go to school before this?"

"A community college in Los Angeles. I wasn't"—I searched for the right words without giving away too much—"sure where I wanted to go, so a local college seemed best last semester."

"I'm glad you're here now. This semester just got a whole lot more interesting."

See? Player. But for some stupid reason, I was all in.

He lifted a wavy strand of my hair, rubbing it between his fingers, his eyes boring into mine. A shiver raced over my body, and he'd only touched my hair.

"Want to go somewhere a little more private?"

So many red flags and warnings went off in my head. It was insanely ridiculous, but I couldn't resist stepping out of my comfort zone and listening to what my body wanted, despite the flares shooting off in my mind. "Yeah, sounds good."

CHAPTER EIGHT

SHANE

Silky strawberry-blond strands hung down Winter's back, brushing along the tops of my hands as I gripped her hips. The press of her body against mine clouded my judgment, and I lost the purpose of bringing her to my room while the party raged on beyond my closed door. Everything about her tempted me physically. Mentally, I was repulsed. The two warred until one outweighed the other.

We stood just inside, and I crowded her against the wall, needing to feel more of her. Craving her. When I touched her, zaps of electricity trailed from the connection and traveled through my body. I bent and brushed my lips against hers. A gasp slipped from her lips, parting them, and I took advantage, deepening the kiss just enough to tease her into wanting more.

My head buzzed, drugged by how good she tasted. When she had nowhere else to go, I cupped her ass and lifted. Her legs automatically wrapped around my waist, and I groaned as I pressed against her heat. Clothes were a fucking barrier I wanted to get rid of. I didn't. Some part of my mind stayed on task.

Lure her in. Seduce her. But don't go too fast. I needed a plan, and I didn't have one yet. She moaned, and my body hardened impossibly more. Just a few more minutes, then I would back off.

How she kissed told me she knew damn well what she was doing. All soft and willing, she was an aphrodisiac. I couldn't get enough. Her tongue tangled with mine, vying for supremacy. When I nipped at her bottom lip and eased the sting with a swipe of my tongue, she moaned and melted against me. I swore the sound went straight to my dick, currently trying to punch out of my pants to get to her.

I held onto one of her jean-clad thighs and cupped the back of her neck with my other hand, my fingers tangled in those soft strands. I wanted to wrap them around my fist and guide my dick past those full, decadent lips. Soon.

I would do so many things with Winter. She had no idea. She didn't even know my name. I'd seen that blank look in her eyes when she'd pretended to remember me. She had no clue who I was, and I would use that to my advantage.

I tugged on her hair, tilting her head to the side and breaking the kiss. With her neck exposed, I pressed open-mouthed kisses along the gentle curve. She squirmed against me, and I swore I saw stars. I'd never wanted to plunge myself so deep into someone as I did her. I had to stay aware and not lose myself in my desire for her. But goddamn, I'd never held someone in my arms that smelled, tasted, or felt as incredible as Winter. I wanted to devour every part of her. In time, I would.

The more I touched her, the harder I found it to extricate myself from her deadly web. She wiggled again, and I groaned. I sucked in air, trying desperately to regain some semblance of composure from the spell she'd wound around me. I was sick. Part of me was dying for more, excited because the girl who'd almost broken me was falling apart in my arms. And this, with her, was the best I'd ever experienced from a simple kiss and some groping. No other girl—not even Tracey—had made me lose my head so fucking fast with a need greater than my will.

With that thought, I tore my lips from her willing body and dropped my forehead to hers. I used my body to hold her in place, my hand tight on her thigh and her hair wound around my fist so she couldn't protest my decision. Our breaths crashed together as we wrestled for control. Seconds passed before my head was clear enough to form a coherent sentence.

I needed a plan, and falling into bed with her right then wasn't it. I wanted her to fall for me, then I would destroy her —*somehow*.

"We hardly know each other." Inside, I cringed at how much of a poser I sounded like. "I don't want to take advantage of you or for you to regret anything."

I shifted to put enough space between us that I could see her expression, thanks to the moonlight spilling through my window. Disappointment registered on her face, but so did a softer emotion. I couldn't tell what, but I liked to think it was gratitude. I already knew she was attracted to me—but I wanted the rest, including her fucking heart and soul.

"Let me walk you home." Because there was no way in hell I wanted her to stick around and have some other asshole hit on her. I'd laid the groundwork, and I would reap the rewards.

"I don't live far. I'll be okay to walk by myself."

"It's not safe. Let me go with."

At her nod, I released her thigh, and her legs slid slowly down my body. I held in my groan at the feel of her. The loss of her body against mine was sheer torture. I threaded our fingers together and tugged her with me.

We left my room, and I led the way so she wouldn't get bumped into. It was still packed inside, and I suspected it would be until almost dawn. Phoenix would have been furious if he were still there. The thought made me smile. I wiped it away as soon as we were outside, on the path, and walking side by side.

"I want to see you tomorrow."

She grinned. "You're seeing me now, and it's almost tomorrow."

"Not what I meant." I squeezed her hand, resisting the urge to twirl her in front of me so I could kiss her again.

We were almost at her dorm. Once I'd found out she roomed with Piper, I knew where she lived. I just needed her number. At the entrance to her building, I turned her toward me, slid my fingers into her back pocket, pinched her phone, and pulled it out.

"What—" She took a hesitant step closer as I held it in front of her face to unlock it.

I put my number in and hit the button to call it. When my phone rang, I hung up. "Now I have your number. Promise to save some time for me soon. I'd like to get to know you better."

Then I cupped her face, tangled my fingers in her hair, and when her lips parted, I kissed her with everything I had. My control was razor-thin, and it took more power than I thought to break the kiss and step away from her. Dilated, dazed green eyes stared intently into mine. Her swollen lips stayed slightly parted. She looked like a goddamn dream. But I knew the truth —she was a fucking nightmare.

I'd taken her ID when I pulled out her phone and used it to swipe the lock on the door. When it buzzed, I pulled it open and held it, handing back her things. "I'll call you tomorrow. Promise to see me then?"

"Mm-hmm." She nodded, spun on her heel, and ducked under my arm to enter the building.

My lips twitched as she walked inside, just as dazed and drugged from my kiss as I felt from touching her. I released the door and turned, only to stop short at the raven-haired beauty before me.

"Who the fuck was that?" Professor Elian hissed.

Where did she come from? I glanced behind Cindy but didn't see a car parked on the side of the road. I straightened to my full height, her voice as effective as a bucket of cold water, dispelling the last traces of Winter's lips.

Her hair hung disheveled around her face, falling to the tops of her shoulders and framing her pale features to accent the lack of her usual red lipstick. I couldn't help but wonder if she had been sleeping with another student nearby. One whose bed she'd just left.

I held my ground, despite wanting to take a step back. "Are you okay?"

Arms crossed, her gaze turned haughty. "No. I'm not. Who the fuck was that girl?" She flung her arm toward the locked glass door to Winter's dorm.

"Just a girl. And how is that any of your business?" I hardened my expression and took a step toward her, towering over her small, curvy frame. "Whatever you think is going on between us, you can forget it. I don't answer to you or any other woman."

"We had plans for this afternoon." A dangerous tremor shook her whispered words.

I huffed, one side of my mouth curving into a mocking grin. "You may have wanted to see me, but I never agreed to meet up with you."

"Because of your new girlfriend."

"Not my girlfriend. Then again"—I loomed over her—"neither are you. It was fun, but I'm no longer interested."

"You forget who I am."

Please. She would be the one to get in trouble, not me. I laughed, and red stained her cheeks.

"We're done. Go home to your husband."

She stepped back before realizing what she'd done then planted her feet firmly where they were. "We're done when I say we are."

"Hardly." I couldn't believe her audacity. I left her standing there to head toward the football house.

We were good together in bed, and I knew I'd made her come more than her husband had probably in all the years they'd been married, but we weren't a thing. It had always been temporary in my mind. Cindy had amazing curves, and she knew what she wanted. I'd liked that. She was bubbly and sexy. But I was bored of her and more than ready to move on.

And since I wasn't her student, she held no power over me.

A cool breeze whipped through the campus, and I shoved my hands in my pockets. The closer I got to the house, the louder it became. No longer in the mood for a party, I changed directions to my SUV. I'd had enough of people for one night.

The night had been hellish hanging out with Winter—kissing her. *How could a kiss with the girl who had tormented me so horrendously spark an almost uncontrollable desire?* If I didn't keep my head in the game, I would be fucked. Then I'd had to deal with Cindy's jealousy on top of it all. I wasn't up for it, not when my mind felt like it'd been put through a shredder.

Once on the road, I drove aimlessly. I had to maintain control when I touched Winter. I couldn't let her affect me like that kiss had. It was the only way. And once she craved me like I was the air she needed to breathe, I would flip the script. I would have my revenge.

I sped by the few vehicles on the highway. It wasn't a clear night. Not even stars or the moon shone overhead—only the glare of car lights and streetlamps. Maybe the beach would be a good option. I could walk along the shore, the waves breaking on the sand, soothing like nothing else. But I wasn't crazy about being alone.

Given the option, I would have gone to Phoenix and Aspen's place. It was late, but I knew Mom would be awake, as it was easier to maintain the same sleeping pattern since she worked nights. She'd mentioned she had the weekend off. Twenty minutes later, I pulled into the driveway where I'd grown up. Several lights were on inside. I used my key and let myself in.

"Mom," I called, not wanting to startle her with the sound of the front door opening.

"In here," she answered from the back of the house.

She was reading in the family room, wearing her favorite pink heart pajama pants and a long-sleeved T-shirt. She closed her book and set it aside, placing her reading glasses on the cover.

I grinned and moved a few of the blue throw pillows out of the way so I could sit on the end of the white couch opposite her. "I thought I would take a chance on you being awake."

"Is everything okay?" Her brows furrowed over eyes the same shade of dark blue as mine. "Is it Phoenix? Or Aspen?"

I held up my hand. "No. Nothing like that. There was a party at the house, and I just felt like coming home instead."

That wasn't completely honest, and I knew she could tell by how she watched me. But she was the best. She always had been. She didn't push. I could sit with her anytime I wanted and not feel pressured to explain my fucked-up state of mind.

"I'm glad you came by." She tucked her dark hair behind her ears, a small smile curving her mouth. "Do you want something to eat?"

"Yeah, that sounds good."

We went into the kitchen, and she pulled out eggs, shredded cheddar cheese, and a bunch of veggies.

After washing my hands, I pushed up my sleeves and got to work chopping the veggies while she beat the eggs. When I was done, I sauteed them while Mom popped in the toast. Once they were cooked enough, Mom got to work at the stove. Not too long after, she slid an omelet onto my plate, followed by toast, then she set butter in front of me with a glass of water.

"You aren't eating?" I paused with my fork hovering over the fluffy omelet, waiting to see if she would join me. "Do you want half of this one?"

"No. I need to sleep soon, and a full stomach always makes that more difficult."

I glanced at the time. It was almost two in the morning. "I thought you had the weekend off."

She gathered the cutting board, knife, and spatula and brought them to the sink, where she washed them. "I was supposed to be off, but Carly got sick, and I said I'd cover her shifts at the hospital."

"Is she on the graveyard shift too?" Switching to a day shift when Mom worked nights would be hard on her system, especially since she'd done nights ever since I could remember. They paid better.

"Yes, or I never would have agreed to it." She leaned against the counter opposite the island.

Devouring the food, I hadn't realized how hungry I was. When I finished, I rinsed my dishes and put them in the dishwasher. I closed it, and she hugged me before pulling back, holding onto my shoulders and looking me in the eyes.

"Is everything okay?"

I forced a smile. "It is. Just adjusting to Phoenix not living in the same house. Things are changing too fast, but I promise, I'm good."

"You'll stay here tonight? I don't want you driving back to Thane this late, especially if you're tired."

"Yeah, I'd planned on it. Thanks, Mom."

She hugged me then said good night before going to her room. I went to mine, feeling the absence of my brother even more. I went to my closet and pulled down the old shoebox where I kept a few things, including the letter I'd written in fifth grade. It had been my big goodbye to the world. I'd kept it all that time because I didn't want to forget how low I'd fallen and had still survived.

I took out the letter, returned the old box to the shelf, and sat on my bed. If it hadn't been for my brother telling me it would kill our mom if I ended things and then Winter moving away so I finally had some peace, I wouldn't be alive. Because of Winter fucking Patten. I couldn't believe I kissed her and managed to keep my hatred hidden.

Back then, Cole, Damon, and my brother had taken me to the gym at our cousins' house. We'd worked out, but what had helped the most was sparring. It was where I'd learned to fight and had later taken those same skills to the Ring. At the time, we'd been too young to fight in the underground fighting ring we'd heard whispers about through a select few people whose brothers were in high school and involved in it.

I'd had a goal and had found my passion outside of football and family. I'd lifted weights, worked out, and learned to fight. And I'd known that when the time was right, I would be in the Ring too.

Everything swirled in my mind. Things had been so exacerbated at that age. Problems were almost impossible, and they'd only gotten worse in junior high. Not long after, I'd found Tracey, who had soothed a part of me that had been irreparably damaged. She was a balm that I didn't think my brother understood. It'd been enough, and when Phoenix had severed that connection with his lie, I'd reacted badly.

The letter crinkled in my hand. But losing Tracey wasn't as devastating as the torment Winter had put me through. Nothing would ever bring me as low as she had. As I shoved the letter into my wallet to carry with me as a reminder, my phone chimed.

Joe's name flashed across the screen, and I tapped the messenger app to open his text. *What the hell is he doing texting me at three in the morning?* That knot in the pit of my stomach grew as I responded. He wanted the money and stated that the house wouldn't stay on the market forever. Someone was sure to snap it up.

I kept my response simple—"I'm working on it."

I wasn't, though. I couldn't go to Grandad. He would disagree, as he hated Joe. I wasn't even sure if Grandad would flip his lid and disown me if he knew I was talking to my dad. It was hypocritical since he'd fucked up in a big way with my brother and Aspen. And that had only happened recently. He'd done plenty before that with his controlling ways, all in the name of love and keeping his family safe. He meant well, but he could be rather extreme about the methods he employed to do so.

With Grandad not an option, the only thing I could think to do was sell my car. Not wanting to deal with another text from Joe, I put my phone on silent and set it on the nightstand. After getting ready for bed, I crawled under the covers and closed my eyes.

I needed to sleep on it, then I would decide. Undoubtedly, going into business with Joe was a bad idea, but he'd offered an olive branch to build a relationship with.

Dammit. I had to find the money. One way or another.

CHAPTER NINE

WINTER

A door slammed, then a body hit the side of my bed. I jolted awake to Piper giggling as she picked herself up off the floor. It was dark in our room, and I squinted at the time— four in the morning. My tension from being woken eased as I tracked her form while she found her bed then flopped face down on it. The stench of stale beer permeated the air. I guessed we weren't going for coffee like she'd said, not with how hungover and passed out she would most likely be all day. Annoyed, I flipped the covers over my head.

Hours later, I showered and ignored the chain saw snoring coming from Piper. I tried to be quiet but quickly realized that it didn't matter. She slept through it all. A sliver of irritation found its way through me at how I'd woken to find the box of Mom's letters I'd stashed under the bed spilled onto the floor between us. Piper must have caught her toe on the edge of it. Even picking them up soured my mood. I didn't want the reminder, especially first thing in the morning.

I glanced around the room at my made bed and laptop that I'd stowed in the still-open middle drawer of my desk after finishing my homework. I slammed it shut and checked to see if

Piper woke. Nope. I doubted even a car crashing through the side of our building could rouse her.

I'd waited long enough. Piper wasn't going to wake up. I needed caffeine desperately, and since my bank account was almost empty, a job wouldn't hurt. I left, catching the door on my way out and closing it so it didn't slam, then took the stairs down to the main floor.

Once outside, I breathed in the fresh air. It was still warm enough out that I was comfortable in jeans and a T-shirt. I tilted my face to the sun, loving the warmth.

With it being Sunday, there weren't as many people out. Most were probably still in bed, sleeping off a hangover or enjoying how they didn't have to wake to an alarm. As I left the campus and, after a few blocks, entered the town, I window-shopped. A bath-and-body store had handmade soaps and lotions in the window. I could smell a hint of lavender when a patron left the shop, the bell jingling overhead. We exchanged smiles, and I moved on. I had no business spending money on things I didn't need.

My walk to the Spot didn't take long. I opened the door and breathed deeply the heavenly scent of roasted beans. The place was packed, as usual. After I placed my order, I asked for a job application and found a seat along the live-edge bar that ran the length of the window to the left of the door.

The buzz of conversation swirled around me as I took my first sip. The caffeine hit my system with a jolt, engaging my brain enough to read over the application. I pulled a pen out of my purse and got to work filling it out. By the time I finished my drink, I'd completed the form and handed it to Becky, the store manager.

I stood there while she skimmed it. She flipped her dark, curly hair over her shoulder with one hand then met my gaze. "You worked as a barista for the last year and a half in Los Angeles?" She smiled at my nod. "When can you start?"

"Anytime." Excitement that it was going well grew inside me. "How about now?"

My brows rose, but I quickly wiped the shock off my features. "Sure."

"Great." Becky's smile widened. "One of our baristas called in sick, and we're short-staffed." She crooked her finger at the cashier with pink cheeks and flyaway hairs sticking out of her drooping ponytail. "Anne here will show you the ropes while I process your application. I just need your driver's license."

I rooted in my purse until I found my ID and handed it to her. Then I dove into bar work, making drinks like I'd worked there for years rather than minutes, and Anne shed the haggardness she'd worn before I'd started. We fell into a rhythm. I lost time, happy that I had a job and some money that would hit my account come payday.

A few more customers came in, and I glanced at the clock. I had another hour on my shift, then I would check in on Piper. I managed pretty well on bar, even with the drinks I had to look up in the recipe book Becky stashed under the counter for me. Or I had managed until he walked in—all mysterious and sexy. My body heated with the memory of being pressed against him as he kissed me last night, and I was instantly distracted.

He filled the entryway. His friends did, too, but I only had eyes for him. The room seemed to shrink from him being there, taking up too much space with his smoldering presence.

I glanced around, noting I wasn't the only one who'd noticed. Girls, and even guys, trailed their every move with intent gazes. I had to tear my gaze from him before the coffee I was making ran over the cup and burned me.

The air felt charged, and my heart raced from anticipation. I sensed the moment his gaze settled on me. My fingers tingled, and my breath came quicker. He affected me entirely too much, but I loved it. That was what I'd missed, and I would definitely let myself experience whatever happened next.

Not only that, but with him there, I wouldn't have to embarrass myself and ask who he was. *Finally, I'll know his name.*

He and the three other guys who had come in with him settled into line, he behind them. Anne took their orders, and when he was up, I tried to be within hearing distance, but the coffee machine was too loud. He placed an order, and when I pulled the ticket off the machine, I had a name to go with the gorgeous guy—*Landon*. Weird, I didn't picture that as his name, not that I had a clue, but whatever. I shook off the odd note that sounded in my mind.

I made the other guys' drinks, which were easy compared to the mocha nonfat, triple shot, with no foam and the other order that were extra.

Another wave of people came in. Anne was fast with taking orders, and I finished up the guys' drinks, set them on the counter, and called their names to pick them up. One by one, they did, all huge guys that I barely paid attention to. They sat at a table off to the left.

The last one, I allowed myself a small break in making drinks. After I made Landon's drink, I set it in front of him at the counter. No one stood in line, for a change, and I flattened my palms on the cool surface. Three tickets waited, but I would get to them shortly.

I spared a minute to take him in—the wicked smirk and mischievous look dancing in his dark-blue eyes told me he had some thoughts where I was concerned too. I wanted to know them.

His large hand curled around the to-go cup. "Thanks, Winter."

I nodded. "Of course."

I glanced at the guys he was with. They looked like football players with similar builds to him.

"When did this happen?" He took a sip of coffee.

"Working here?" A half grin curved my lips. "This morning. I needed a job, and this one gives me direct access to a steady stream of caffeine."

"Guess I'll have to come in more often."

I laughed. Movement from the corner of my eye had me straightening and stepping away from the counter. "I'll talk to you later." No matter how much I wanted to stay there and chat with him, it wouldn't look good since Becky had just walked out of her office.

His gaze slid to where mine had been, and he took the hint, going to the table with his friends.

I busied myself with wiping things down between new orders. When it was time to take my break, I grabbed my purse and snuck a peek at my phone. A message from Landon asked when I would get off my shift. My stomach flipped as I typed out a response then hit send.

When I returned to the bar and stowed my purse, I caught him looking at his screen before our eyes met, and the smile that curved his lips held a promise that I couldn't wait to cash in.

CHAPTER TEN

SHANE

The guys I came to get coffee with had left, and I spent the next few minutes leaning against the side of the building, waiting for Winter's shift to end. The bell over the door jingled, and I glanced up and found Winter exiting.

Everything about her appealed to me. From her slender, graceful build to her gorgeous face and long, wavy hair. I had to keep in mind that behind the lovely façade, she was deceptively deadly. I forced my mouth to relax. I hadn't stuttered in years, and I refused to start again because of her. The goodbye letter to my family, from when I was at my lowest, lent an imaginary weight to my pocket. Still stashed in my wallet, it served as a reminder of Winter's capability.

That time in my past was embarrassing and humiliating. The present Winter seemed different from the one I'd known. It was a fucking act. And even though I hadn't known why she'd left town when we were young—because I'd been wrapped up in my own pain—I was glad she had because, at that point, the relief had been overwhelming.

I shoved my phone in my pocket when she turned my way, her dazzling smile almost knocking the air from my lungs. My fingers curled, but I forced them to relax at my sides, refusing to give in to the urge to touch her. I had to remember she deserved everything I planned to dish out—the lies, the fake name Landon, and ultimately, making her fall in love with me only to watch me walk away.

"How was your first barista shift?" I pushed away from the wall, and we fell into step together, heading toward campus.

"It was good but long. I like Becky, the manager, and Anne. I haven't met any other coworkers yet."

"I'm sure you will soon. Are you scheduled to work a lot?" I threaded our hands together as we continued on the sidewalk. "Because I'll have to drink more coffee, then."

"I'll only be there a few days a week. They have a large staff. It was just that someone called in sick today, and Becky asked if I could start immediately, so…"

"Right time, right place."

"Exactly." She smiled, and her face lit up. "What do you have going on today? No practice?"

"It's Sunday." I could have used practice, though. I needed to keep my mind focused. "A bunch of guys and I watched film then went to the gym and lifted. Besides that, it's a homework and study catch-up day."

"Oh, I forgot what day it was. The weekend goes by way too fast."

As we turned a corner, I had to slow my pace to match hers. "It does. And if I didn't have two tests next week, it wouldn't be so bad."

"Want to hit the library tonight?" Winter tucked a strand of hair behind her ear, and I followed the movement with my eyes. "I have a paper to write, and it would be easier to do it there than in my room."

"I'm heading off campus after we get to your dorm. I have a family thing."

Her brows furrowed as she turned to meet my gaze. "You didn't have to wait for me, then."

"I wanted to." I ran my thumb over the back of her hand. We stopped in front of her building, and I turned her to me then tucked a strand of her hair behind her ear. "I'll message you if I get back early." My hand lingered on the side of her face. Before dropping it back to my side, I brushed my thumb over her full bottom lip.

When she sucked in a breath, I felt like I'd scored the winning touchdown.

Rather than kiss her, I would leave her wanting more. "I'll catch you later."

I turned at her soft goodbye, my ears straining for when she broke free from my spell and walked inside. And there it was. I had to stifle a laugh because my plan was taking root.

Following the sense of satisfaction, a wave of remorse blind-sided me. Luke's death was never far from my thoughts. While the kid had been a problem, he didn't deserve to die. I cringed as I saw it all over again—the solid connection of my fist to his jaw, the way his eyes rolled back into his head, how his body had melted and the thud of his head against that damn concrete step, his neck at an awkward angle, and the pool of blood and yellow spinal fluid seeping onto the concrete.

Those few seconds haunted my dreams and invaded my thoughts with soul-crushing frequency. Planning and plotting against Winter helped keep me from drowning, serving as a reprieve from the guilt of ending Luke's life.

I adjusted my baseball hat low over my forehead. I couldn't do much to disguise who I was, not with my height and build, but I tried to be inconspicuous. Some people stared as I passed, which I knew was because of what had been printed about Luke and me in the papers. Though I loathed reading them, I had to in case I got linked to the underground fights. With each passing day, a tiny amount of tension about that coming to light and my future going to hell worse than it already had eased the continuous pressure around my lungs.

Coach hadn't kicked me off the team since it was ruled as self-defense and the police had dropped the charges. It wasn't what Luke's family wanted, but the ruling should stand unless they brought more evidence—like the underground fights. Or that was what my uncle had said, and Grandad's lawyer had agreed.

Between that and the constant reminder of how Winter had treated me, I wasn't getting much sleep. I unlocked my SUV, got in, and prepared to deal with the next giant fucking hurdle—meeting Joe at Dillon's. The paperwork from the bank Grandad used sat on the passenger seat, mocking me. I had to convince Joe the loan was the best course of action. Then maybe I could begin to heal the rift between him and my family.

It wasn't quite dinnertime, which made parking easier. I found a spot, grabbed the paperwork, and headed into the diner. The bell jingled loudly over the door, and I slid into an empty booth to wait for Joe. A glance at the time showed he was late. The waitress brought water, but I told her I would wait to order.

I wasn't sure how the meeting would go. He'd been pushing hard for his business idea, and I wasn't sure he would be open to doing things differently. Plus, I liked my SUV, and I didn't want to sell it, especially since Grandad had demanded to hold the title, claiming that my brother and I weren't responsible enough when Uncle Lucas had given me the vehicle. It was also the only way he would allow my uncle to do anything, like buy us the SUVs. Grandad had too much bad blood with my uncle, who was related through marriage to my late aunt.

While waiting, I messaged Phoenix to see how Aspen was doing. It was still so weird that my brother was married and had a kid on the way. Good thing I liked Aspen—now. I hadn't in the past, but we were mostly over that. There had been too many changes. My brother was shooting for an early draft into the NFL in his third year of college. I got it, but that wasn't my path. I wanted to focus on my degree. I would miss the hell out of him because he would definitely get picked up in the first round. He was that good. I was, too, but Phoenix was fucking phenomenal.

The door opened, and I glanced in its direction as Joe walked in, spotted me, and headed over. His hair was freshly buzzed, and while he was still built like an athlete at forty, his face looked haggard and put him closer to his midfifties. Phoenix and I hadn't liked how he'd aged, as it might not bode well for us. Mom looked young, though, and I'd teased Phoenix that since I took after her in looks—just hair and eye color—I wouldn't look like an old man at forty but he would. Joe slid into the booth, and I pushed aside my thoughts about teasing my brother.

"Do you have the check?"

Hello to you too. "No, but I brought these." I slid the loan papers over to him.

Joe leaned back, his eyes taking on a hard glint. "That's disappointing. I would have thought you would put your heart into this. We could be Wrenshall & Sons Construction, a family legacy." He shook his head.

Tension shot through my body, but I kept my face blank, refusing to broadcast that his misguided assessment got to me. "Maybe if you would look at the papers I brought, we could discuss going a different direction." He held my gaze and didn't look down. "It's an application for a small business loan."

"I can't go the bank route due to my credit history." He leaned forward, his forearms braced on the table. "I should've realized that you wouldn't know anything about a hard day's work after being raised by your mother and grandfather. Your grandfather made it clear that he would provide everything for you both, but what he did was a disservice. Now, you boys don't know how to sacrifice."

I clenched my jaw so hard I wouldn't be surprised if a few molars cracked. Mouth pressed in a line, I said nothing. I'd embarrassed him; I could see that. It wasn't that I was opposed to the business he'd proposed. It would complement Grandad's property management company, and I bet I could establish a profitable arrangement between the two companies. But the money and my time were a problem. As were his impatience and defensiveness.

Joe waited for another beat then stood. "Call me when you're serious about starting the business and you have a check in hand. This could be a great thing for our family. Healing even." Then he walked out of the diner.

My hands curled into fists on top of my thighs. That was manipulation at its best, and I was the sucker who would cave to it. I swiped the papers from the table and hauled myself out of the booth. I hated the position he had just put me in. And I fucking loved my car but not more than my family. Grandad was a headache, but he loved us in his own screwed-up way. At least with him, I knew he would always have our backs, even if he went about things in the wrong way.

But when it came to Joe, no matter how much I knew I should go to Grandad, I couldn't. He hated Joe a hundred times more than the misconstrued perception of Uncle Lucas's influence over our aunt's decisions and the tragic end of her life. That meant Uncle Lucas had some redeeming qualities in Grandad's eyes, and Joe did not.

Before I did anything, I went to see my brother. Phoenix opened the door to his and Aspen's apartment. I looked around at how comfortable they'd made it and felt gutted again that I hadn't been there to help them move in because I was bodyguarding Erica.

It wasn't big, but they'd done a lot with it. Aspen's hand-painted surfboards were mounted along one wall. A comfortable couch sat facing the TV. The room opened to the tiny kitchen with a peninsula where they could eat. They had two small bedrooms and a bathroom. Aspen spent a lot of time painting her surfboards on their patio just through the kitchen.

"Where's Aspen?"

"Drawing with Max. She'll be back soon." Phoenix shut the door behind me. "Thanks for coming by."

"You're being weird. Since when do you have to thank me for coming over? You're my brother."

His mouth pressed in a straight line, hitting me like a punch to the gut. He had a point. I hadn't been there for him recently. So much shit had gone on in my head after the breakup with Tracey, which I'd blamed him for. It was his fault, but it would have happened eventually. I knew I needed to cut her loose. I just hadn't wanted to. She'd gotten me over a big hurdle, and I'd finally gained some much-needed confidence. Because of that, I cut her some slack.

Mentally, I was a mess—even more so because Joe had made contact and I'd kept it from my brother.

"I need to talk to you about Joe," Phoenix said.

I sat on one of the stools at the peninsula and got comfortable. It wasn't going to go well. I could already tell from the muscle that jumped along Phoenix's jaw and his closed-off vibe. "Okay. Shoot."

"You know I hate Joe. He's never had a relationship with us, and even if you're willing to, I'm not going to entertain one with him."

My brother resembled Joe in many ways, but just in looks. Phoenix had qualities that Joe could not attain because he'd already violated them: trust and loyalty. They were the most important in family. I could always count on my brother. And he had a right to feel the way he did about Joe, regardless of what I knew or how Joe was trying to make things right with me.

"With a baby on the way, it's the worst time to forge a new relationship with someone I've hated since I can remember. It's not my focus—that's Aspen, the baby, and our future."

My elbows thumped on the counter. "I get it. Your priorities should be on your family, school, and football." It was different for me. I didn't have a girlfriend, and my future was uncertain.

"And you." His silver eyes blazed. "I want you right there with me. Are you worried about the Green family retaliating, though they don't have a case against you?"

A chill passed over me. The mention of Luke alone seemed to resurrect him from the recesses of my mind, where he lurked, waiting to attack me with the memories of what I'd done. "I am, but leave it alone. I don't want you near the Greens or me if something happens."

"That's bullshit." That same muscle jumped furiously along his jaw. "What happens to you happens to me. We're twins. You don't think I feel the shit you're going through?"

Goddammit. "Phoenix." I closed my eyes briefly, struggling to control my emotions. "You have too much on the line. I've got Grandad and Uncle Lucas fighting for me. You know they would never let anything happen."

"I hate it. This shouldn't be happening."

My gut churned. "I know. I was stupid."

"No. Not that. Just… it was an accident. You shouldn't be facing any repercussions."

He meant a civil case, and I wasn't sure I was out of the woods there. Though I wished for the same exoneration he spoke of. "I don't want to talk about it right now."

"Fine." Phoenix yanked open the fridge, grabbed an apple, and tossed it to me before taking one for himself. "What bullshit is Joe feeding you?"

I grimaced as he transitioned from one emotionally charged

subject to the next. "Come on, man. Let's drop both of those conversations. It's too damn early in the day for them."

"Coach told me how many invites Thane has for the combine."

"Holy fuck. Did you get an invite?"

"He's not releasing that yet, but we got thirteen. That's a high number for a D1 school."

"The fucking combine." It was a week-long, on-field event to test athleticism and conduct interviews for the NFL. "You'll get one for sure."

He shrugged. "It's too early, and we both know it. But Cole."

Cole was a year older. It was possible. "Did he declare?"

"Not yet. He wants to finish college with Riley before he declares his intent to enter the NFL draft. Especially since the next Olympics isn't until after they graduate."

That made sense. Once he declared, he wouldn't be eligible to play for college. "He'll do it his senior year."

"Yeah."

"What about you?"

"I don't know." He took a bite of his apple then set it down. "I already talked to Aspen about it. But I want to. You know school is…"

"I get it." He had mild dyslexia, so he had to work hard and needed someone to read the assignments or whatever wasn't available on audio. "I thought you wanted to finish college, though. For a backup plan."

"I do. I will. But… with the baby."

"It's not a bad idea. It would set you guys up, and she's got her custom surfboard website going."

"Yeah, she's killin' it. It's good that Skylar, Cass, and Riley are helping with pictures and marketing."

Skylar was Damon's girlfriend. Riley was Cole's, and Cass was their friend who had gone to high school with us.

"I thought you would wait until our third year to declare." I'd made peace with that when he'd told me. If I was still eligible, I planned to declare senior year and follow only a year behind him. But I wanted to get my degree. I would still need my master's, but I could work on it in the off season. It would just take a while. If—and it was a big if with everything going on—I was still eligible and not in jail.

"I was going to wait, but with the baby coming soon, I think I'll go for it next year instead."

"How does Aspen feel about it? Will she go with you when you're drafted? Or finish school here? 'Cause you know we'll all help her with the baby. She won't be alone. And you guys are moving into the house Cole is buying for us just off campus." Panic crawled up my spine. I didn't even know why. Maybe because I didn't want to face what my future would look like without my brother. If he were in the NFL, he wouldn't be there. It was selfish. I got that. And I hated myself for hoping Phoenix would wait to go.

It wasn't even a question if he would be drafted. My brother had eyes on him every time he played. He was that good.

"Aspen has her business." Phoenix glanced at the surfboards she'd painted and he'd mounted along the far wall. "It's already succeeding. She's on board with me declaring next year."

"I'm happy for you. What team are you hoping for?"

He grinned, all the tension that'd bracketed his mouth melting away. "I want to stay in California. The Chargers will need a quarterback, Bernard isn't renewing his contract. Rumor is he's retiring."

"I'll have to keep an eye on their defense." I wanted to be on the same team as my brother. If that wasn't possible, then the 49ers. "What about Cole and Damon? I haven't checked in with them lately."

"I don't know what teams they're monitoring. But back to *you* not knowing." Phoenix's eyes narrowed. "You've been MIA, which is understandable, but knock it off. We all care."

It didn't need to be said. Our cousins always had our backs. We grew up together and were more brothers than cousins. "I need to work off some frustration, and since I can't do the fights anymore, I wanted to see if you or they were game to spar."

"Always. You know that." He bent, elbows on the counter, and leaned closer. "What's really going on with you?"

"I'm good." I blocked him as best as I could, but my brother had an inside track—our connection. "I just need the outlet, that's all."

"I'm calling bullshit."

"Doesn't matter. It's a waiting game right now. You know that."

"I don't like it. We should do something to make it go away."

I snorted. "Like what? Intimidate Luke's parents? You know we wouldn't do that. They lost their kid. They're more than entitled to deal with it however they see fit."

"Not when it comes to you."

Everything fell away, and I knew he saw the darkness in me by how tense he got. "Even when it comes to me."

The door opened, saving me from my brother's inquisition. Aspen walked in with her best friend, Max, who dumped her bag on the coffee table. He hugged her, shouted hi to us, and headed out.

"Where's Max off to?" Phoenix asked as Aspen came closer.

She patted me on the shoulder then went to my brother and looped her arms around his neck. Everything in him softened, and I ached for what they had. She was the epitome of a surfer chick. Sun-streaked blond hair, laid-back and happy vibe, golden tan, and toned everywhere from spending so much time in the water. Her blue eyes sparkled, and my brother melted whenever she was near.

"Max is meeting Jaxon but might return when you're working out later."

Phoenix kissed her then dropped his hands to her baby

bump. They shared grins, and Aspen laughed before waving me over. "Come here, Shane. The baby's kicking."

I got up and went over, putting my hand where Aspen indicated. A soft bump pushed against her firm belly. It was the coolest thing I'd ever felt, and I laughed. "That's incredible. I can't wait to meet her."

"Hopefully, not too soon," Phoenix said.

He was worried.

I hit him in the shoulder. "Aspen's got this. Stop stressing."

I felt the snort that followed my comment. I would've been a wreck, too, had it been my wife and our first baby.

"Next year will be fun," I said, staying positive. They didn't need any more stress with the load they'd already shouldered. "All of us in one house and me being the favorite uncle."

I stayed for another half hour, catching up and deciding against bringing up why I'd stopped by—Joe and the business he wanted to go into with us.

I got in my SUV after hanging with Phoenix and Aspen and headed toward the closest car dealership. I shouldn't even be contemplating it, but I was the family's peacekeeper, and I couldn't think of another way around it since Joe had refused to even look at the loan application.

My hands gripped the steering wheel tight, the miles disappearing beneath my tires too quickly. Before I knew it, I was in the car dealer's lot and in front of a salesperson. In a dark-blue suit and a striped tie, the man with dark, slicked-back hair and bushy eyebrows greeted me with dollar signs in his eyes.

"Welcome to Stan's Dealership. I'm Tim. How can I help you?"

His wore a wide smile, and I swore he smelled a sale in the air, detecting a sucker—*that's me.*

The Range Rover was worth a lot of money, especially since Uncle Lucas had spared no expense when he'd purchased the top-of-the-line models with all the bells and whistles for his sons and nephews.

My gut churned, and it hurt to force the words out. "What can I get for this?"

"Is this yours?" Tim opened the door, glancing inside.

"Yes." *Fuck, this is hard.*

"I'll have our mechanic look it over, then I can quote you. Do you have the title?"

"Not on me." *Could I even get it from Grandad? Not likely.*

"Okay, well, if you bring it back tomorrow after our mechanic has a chance to look it over, I can cut you a check. Do you need a less expensive car? I have a sweet deal on the Dodge Charger."

I glanced to where he'd pointed but couldn't even see the muscle car with how sick my stomach felt. "Thanks, man. I can't leave the SUV now, but I'll return with the title."

If I even had a chance of prying it out of Grandad's hands. *But what other choice do I have?*

CHAPTER ELEVEN

WINTER

After a less-than-stellar dinner at the café on campus, I headed to the library. I'd left my phone behind in the dorms after obsessively checking to see if Landon had messaged. Ridiculous. I had way too much to do to be fixating on a boy—even if he was sinfully hot.

I promised myself I would let my guard down and let others in. But the distraction wasn't helping me get work done. So, phoneless, I slung my backpack over my shoulder and walked across campus.

Once inside, I took in the spacious interior filled with wall-to-wall books, standing bookcases, and scattered tables. Thane's library was incredible, and the urge to find a few romance books and curl up with them instead of my homework was almost too great to resist. I promised myself that if I finished everything, I could browse the fiction section and find a new one to take home. It was a hidden indulgence I didn't like to share with others. Brooke knew, and Jaxon because he stole them from my room, but not James, my foster dad. That would have been embarrassing.

I found a quiet table on the second floor in the back corner, pulled out my laptop, and worked on my paper. Two hours later, I had it written, read through, and submitted to my professor.

The days were shorter, and the sun had gone down by the time I glanced out the window. It was dark outside, which would make walking through campus to my dorm suck, but at least the pathways were well lit and usually had a few students doing the same thing. No matter how much I wanted to call it a night, I had that other unpleasant thing to research first.

With Mom's parole date fast approaching and my memory absolute shit, I needed to read through the old newspaper articles on microfilm from when everything had gone to hell. Then, I could figure out what to do.

I shoved everything in my backpack and found one of the library computers to search through old newspaper articles around the time my sister had died and my mom had gone to trial then jail. I typed the date ranges and her name in the search bar, then I closed my eyes and let the computer do its thing while I got lost in my sparse memories of the past.

My recall was mostly hazy from that day at the lake house. Summer and I had been there before. Mom would drag us to the lake and leave us outside by the creaky dock until she was done doing whatever she did inside the house. All Summer and I knew was that we weren't allowed inside, even if we had to pee. Too bad.

Summer and I were throwing rocks we'd collected and brought onto the dock. We were facing the water, away from the house. I remembered hearing Mom's voice. She was angry and too close. Pain exploded across my back, but it was nothing compared to the fear. An ear-piercing scream split the air. I had no idea if it came from my sister or me. Then the water.

Neither of us could swim. That was where things turned murkier in my mind. I remembered opening my eyes and coughing. I lay on the coarse, rocky ground at the edge of the water, struggling to fill my lungs, Beside me, my sister lay sprawled, soaking wet, small stones stuck to her cheek, and unmoving. Then nothing. My brain remained blank no matter how hard I tried to remember. And I'd tried. Over and over again.

I snapped out of it as one article after another loaded on the monitor. Nausea swirled in my stomach as I skimmed them. The details were sketchy. My sister's murder had happened at McMillan Lake, on the outskirts of the subdivision where I'd lived with my family. Mom was the only suspect, and Summer and I had been alone at the lake when our mother had come out of the cabin. The police believed Katrina Patten had pushed us into the water. She'd maintained that someone else had been there.

None of the articles listed another potential suspect, and only one referenced Mom saying a man had been there. She'd never named him, and no other witnesses could place anyone other than the three of us there.

People in Santa Monica knew about my sister's murder. It had been headline news, and the trial, a public spectacle. However, I had little memory of it. I only knew that I'd told the police Mom had pushed us into the water.

With my head pounding and a sense that everything would inevitably implode with her upcoming parole hearing, I closed the articles and slung my backpack over my shoulder. A quick stop in the romance section and a book secured in my bag, and I was out the door. I'd had enough. Anything dealing with my mom or my sister's death destroyed me.

Outside, the fresh air helped get me out of the funk reading the articles had put me in. Rain was expected late that night, and the warm air and the cold front had ushered in a dense fog. It surrounded me, making the faint glow from the streetlamps hazy. The way the fog pressed in around me offered comfort, despite the unnerving shadows when someone neared on the sidewalk. A few feet before we crossed paths, their shape and features took form.

When I opened the door to my dorm, my clothes were damp. Rain would probably come sooner than what had been forecasted. I shoved my hair from my face, looking forward to the sound of raindrops against the window.

I climbed the stairs, then halfway down the hall, I let myself into my room with my key. Piper sat in the middle of her bed with books spread around her. A pencil stuck out from the messy blond bun she'd twisted her hair into on top of her head.

"Finally, you're back." Her lips pressed tightly together as she flung down the pen she'd been writing with.

"Ah, yeah. I would have gone to get coffee with you as planned, but you were passed out."

She waved her hand. "I was—am—hungover. I wouldn't have been great company. Sorry about that."

"Okay, so, what's with the 'finally'?" I set my bag on my desk chair.

"It's your phone. It's been ringing like crazy. I silenced it, but it's still vibrating and annoying." She rubbed her temples. "Sorry, just feeling like crap."

I offered a small smile. I could imagine. I didn't drink, but it wasn't like I didn't know what a hangover did to people. I looked around for my phone, as it wasn't where I'd left it on my desk.

"I put it under your pillow."

"Thanks." I couldn't blame her. If I were trying to get homework done and her phone was ringing like crazy, I would have been irritated too. I checked the number, worried it might be Brooke trying to get ahold of me.

No contact name, just a number—but I recognized it. *Landon.* My heart fluttered. My phone buzzed, displaying the same number while I was holding it, and I answered.

"Hey."

"Winter?" His deep voice sent goose bumps racing over my skin. "It's Landon."

"I recognized your number." I smiled.

"I was worried when you didn't answer."

Right, he'd told me he would call later if he could study. And my obsessively checking my phone was why I'd left it in the room. "I forgot my phone in my room when I went to the library."

"You're done with your paper?"

"I am." I bit my bottom lip to keep me from rambling about anything else.

"Do you want to get out for a little while, go for ice cream?"

"Yeah, I would love that."

"Great." I could hear the smile in his voice. "I'll pick you up in five minutes."

"Okay. See you soon."

I hung up, and Piper tore her gaze from her computer. "Hey" —she waved toward her desk—"I grabbed those from the RA's room."

A handful of condoms filled a small dish on the corner of her desk. "Interesting."

She laughed. "He keeps a candy bowl full of them for anyone on the floor. Just wanted to let you know they're there in case you need 'em spur of the moment, because you never know..." She wiggled her eyebrows.

I laughed. "Thanks. I'm heading out for a little while."

"'Kay. See ya." Her head was already down, her words distracted by whatever she was reading.

I grabbed my keys and went to the lobby to wait for Landon. With a minute or two until he arrived, I went to my mailbox to see if I'd received anything. A single white piece of paper lay inside, folded up but with my name on it.

It was folded into three sections. I unfolded the top part, and my head swam from the single word in red pen, all caps—*killer*.

My body felt weak as I opened the note with trembling hands and found the same red ink. My eyes swam with tears at what was printed.

I know what you did.

CHAPTER TWELVE

SHANE

I ended the call to Winter and shoved my phone into my pocket. Irritation trailed my every move. I didn't have time to take her out for ice cream. Too many things had been in the air lately. I combed a hand through my hair, resolve settling over me like a heavy blanket. I was going to do it for a reason. It'd been eight years since she'd shaken my confidence to dangerous levels, and it was time to exact my revenge. *Getting back at her is one of the things I want to handle.* The rest of my long list of tasks could wait.

"What the hell was that about?"

I craned my neck around the corner of the football house's family room as Damon approached from the kitchen. He looked at me like I was crazy, and I frowned.

"Why are you pretending to be someone named Landon?"

It was a rare night when the room wasn't packed with housemates playing video games or making food. A few guys filled the kitchen, and I knew it would only be a matter of time before they invaded my current space. What I would share with my cousin wasn't a story I wanted someone to overhear, so I got to the meat of it quickly.

"Do you remember Winter Patten from fifth grade?"

Damon sat on the opposite end of the couch and ate his sandwich, his brows scrunched. "Not offhand. Why?"

I thought back to that time and remembered a few more things. "You hung around with Joey Leary back then and played a lot of basketball."

"Oh, right." Damon grinned. "I thought I should do something other than what my brother was into. It was a competitive year between us."

I laughed. "Shit. I forgot about that. You got angry in that pickup football game we were playing at recess. You shouted at Cole that he sucked and couldn't run a route if he was the only one on the field."

"Yeah. I was kind of a dick back then." The laughter vanished from Damon. "Our parents were always fighting, and Cole told me off a few times about Mom when I sided with Dad. We didn't have the same perspective."

"Only then?" I grinned. They had always been tight. But I remembered how much their parents' fights wore on them. It had been terrible that year. Not that it got better, but it was the beginning of the end. Their home life, football, and girls had consumed them. Anyone else's problems, other than mine or my brother's, didn't even hit their radar.

He smirked. "You were acting weird most of the time, super shy, and Cole and I were fighting about our parents. But what made me tackle him and give him a bloody nose that day was because he kissed Sarah McQueen, and he knew I wanted to go for her."

"You did anyway."

Damon snorted. "Good times."

The guys grew louder in the kitchen, and the microwave dinged. "Winter was the girl with long strawberry-blond hair. She moved away during fifth grade, but she made my life hell before she did."

"What? I don't remember any of that."

"You don't remember when she told our entire class that I had a tiny dick and that I broke my arm jerking off?"

"Oh, shit!" Damon's blue eyes danced with mirth. "I do remember that. You didn't break it, though."

"Nope. I fell out of the palm tree and sprained it."

Damon kicked his feet onto the coffee table. "It's weird that I don't remember her. So, that's who you were talking to?"

"She transferred here this semester and didn't remember me." Darkness swirled, and I clenched my hands, fighting the urge to hit something. Maybe Damon.

It was such a fucked-up time for me. But to be fair, my brother was the only one who knew. I'd sworn him to secrecy about how much I was struggling. Even against his wishes to bring our cousins in on it. "And since she doesn't, I thought it would be a good time for payback."

Damon studied me for a couple of seconds then seemed to come to a decision. "Whatever's going on, if you need me for anything, I've got your back."

"I know you do." So did both our brothers. Nothing could come between us. I grabbed my keys from where I'd tossed them on the table and stood. "I'm heading out. I'll catch you later."

Fifth grade through eighth was a weird time for most people, but out of our group, it'd been especially so for me. It wasn't until high school that things had changed. I'd gotten stronger, and nothing could pull me back down to that low time in my life. I'd finally conquered it and was better. Tracey had played a large part in that, until she hadn't. How we parted ways, it'd torn me up, but it hadn't broken me. Nothing would again, not ever. I was better than that.

I'd loosely formed my plan with a tangible end goal. I just needed to get to know her to find her weak, most vulnerable spots. I wanted to deliver a strike that would cripple her.

I got into my Range Rover, drove to her dorm, parked in front of the building, and waited for her to come out. I didn't wait long. She jogged out in jeans and a tight blue T-shirt, her long hair rippling behind her.

Then she yanked open the door and climbed in, her face pale and hands trembling.

What happened since we hung up? I didn't care, but I needed her to think I did, so I played the part. "What's wrong?"

"I'm just… uh, I don't know. I think someone's following me."

"Why do you think that?" I turned in my seat, not bothering to put the SUV in park. It would come across better if I gave her my undivided attention.

She blew out a breath and looked back at her building. "I-I don't really want to talk about it. Just a feeling I had." She turned back to me and forced a bright smile that didn't reach her eyes.

I made myself take her hand and held her gaze. "If someone's a problem for you, let me know. I can help."

Her lower lip trembled before she got control of herself. "Thanks. I'm sure it's nothing."

"If you're sure." I waited for her to nod before I pulled away from the curb and pointed us toward the ice cream shop.

I drove for the next few minutes with classic rock playing on the radio and filling the silence until I found a parking spot on the street not far from Scoops, the favored ice cream shop by Thane's students. We went inside the well-lit interior and placed our orders for single-serving cups, rather than cones. With a scoop each of ice cream, turtle for me and mocha almond fudge for her, we found a small table near the back.

The hum of conversation swirled around us as we took a few bites. Some color had returned to her face, and her shoulders didn't look as tight.

"You mentioned you went to another school for a semester before transferring. Was that because of family?"

Spoon halfway to her mouth, she paused. "In part. I liked living at home and wasn't looking to go away to school."

Unusual. Everyone I knew couldn't wait to get away, myself included. "But you changed your mind."

"Mm-hmm." Her eyes flicked to the left before returning to me. "What about you? Did you always want to go to Thane?"

"Yes." I didn't elaborate. Talking about myself was not the goal, and it was risky. "What was so great about hanging at home?"

A genuine smile curved her full lips. "Brooke liked to go for walks, and she would always drag me and Jax along or whoever was home."

"Brooke?"

"Brooke and James are my foster parents. Jax is their son."

Foster parents? What the hell did I miss? "Wait. Aren't you eighteen or nineteen?"

"Nineteen, and I did age out of the system. It never mattered to my foster family. If they could have, they would have adopted me. Brooke has always said I'm their daughter, and having a piece of paper say so doesn't mean anything to them. They treat me like one of their own, and I appreciate them so much for it."

I nodded. That was new information. *Or did I know that about her?* I didn't think so. "So, the walks and just being with them then?" I sort of got that. My mom was amazing, but Cole and Damon used to have issues with their parents.

"We did a lot together. Going to the beach. Brooke loves to cook, and she would rope Jax and me into helping her in the kitchen." She shrugged, pink staining her cheeks. "It was fun and nothing I'd experienced before. I didn't have a reason to want to leave."

"Then why did you?" I scooped the last of my ice cream onto the spoon and ate it.

She pushed out a breath, her eyes sliding away for a second. "It was something I needed to do."

"Why weren't they able to adopt you?"

Her smile was tight. "What about you? Do you have any brothers or sisters?"

Huh, I'd hit on a touchy subject. Interesting. Rather than push, I went with the subject change. "I have an older brother." *By two minutes, but she doesn't need to know that.*

"Does he go here, too, or a different college?"

"For now, he's here. How's it going living with Piper?"

Her gaze sharpened when I changed the subject. I knew she wouldn't push it because she'd done the same.

"Piper is great. We don't have any issues being roommates, and the friendship part will come. I'm not worried. Plus Jaxon is here if I ever get lonely."

I let her see desire as I fixed her with a heat-filled stare. "You've got me." It was calculated, but she didn't need to know that.

The pink returned to her cheeks, and she shifted in her seat.

I teased her the rest of the night and got her to laugh. I had no intention of taking things any further and dropped her off at her dorm with a kiss that I refused to let go anywhere, not yet anyway.

Back at the football house, I went to my room and powered up my laptop. My single focus was Winter. I had no energy to worry about Joe or Grandad or the car right then. I needed to find out why she'd left and what she had been up to since she'd been gone because I didn't believe a goddammed word that came out of her mouth.

I typed her last name and Santa Monica into the search engine, hoping that would narrow things down. Articles flooded the page about a murder trial involving Katrina Patten. I clicked on the first one and settled in to read everything I could find.

An hour later, I still couldn't believe it. It seemed as if Winter and I had something in common. Sort of. She hadn't committed the crime. I had. But murder ran in her family too. Her sister's murder specifically, and her mom had gone to jail for it.

Holy fuck. How did I not remember that? It'd been a big deal at the time. I shut my laptop and leaned back in my chair, clasping my hands behind my neck. Her mom going to jail was why Winter had left—and why my life had improved significantly.

A small part of me felt bad for her, but that was before I found an obscure post that speculated whether Winter had been the one to kill her sister and not her mom. That sounded about right with how cruel she'd been back then. I could believe it of her easily. She might pretend she was different, but I remembered every dark thing she'd done to tear me down and leave me out on the edge, hanging on by my fucking fingertips. So, no. I wouldn't go easy on her.

Though I couldn't remember details about the trial or what had happened to her, I knew someone who would—my mom. I would check in with her tomorrow. My reading had helped me develop a plan. *I'll get every grisly detail about her past and post it on social media.*

It was late when I sent out the group text to my brother and cousins. I couldn't sleep, and the gym would be mostly empty, so I headed there and waited. It wasn't long before they showed up.

Cole and Damon entered the gym and went to the mats where Phoenix and I were stretching. The punching ball and a bag weren't in the way where we planned to spar. Unlike what we were used to when we did it back home, the gym wasn't private. But we sparred together, and it helped with the anger we each carried.

Our cousins, not as much. Phoenix had changed after the accident, but he had worries of his own, and it was a great outlet when football or sex wasn't enough. Then there was me. I was a fucking wreck. I needed it like my next breath.

"I'm surprised Sky and Riley let you two out," I teased.

"Shut the fuck up." Laughing, Damon cracked me in the back of the head.

Cole grunted then dropped his bag. "We gonna do this?"

He leveled his stare my way, and I jumped to my feet. "Yeah, I'm first."

We took a minute to tape our hands, flexing them to ensure they weren't too tight. Before long, we sparred, circling one another and exchanging punches, working up a sweat. It felt good to burn off some excess energy and do something with my cousins and brother.

I stayed constant in the ring while Cole swapped out with Damon then Phoenix went in last. Two hours later, my arms were almost too heavy to lift, but I felt lighter than I had in a long while, and I felt confident I would pass out when I got back to my room. I needed it.

Damon smacked me on the back, grinning. "We need to do this more often. Football clearly isn't enough."

"Yeah, once or twice a week if we can manage it," I agreed. "How's Sky doing?" Damon's girlfriend wrote for the school paper and was on the editorial team. I didn't see the girls enough.

"Busy with classes. I tried to get her to cover sports again."

"You're an idiot." Cole snorted. "She won't give you more space in the article or brag about how awesome you are."

"Yeah, she would. I would withhold orgasms until she did." Damon winked. "We've already had this discussion. I would win."

"She'd kick your ass is what would happen." Phoenix tossed his wadded-up hand tape at Damon.

Sky wasn't easily intimidated and had a quick wit. It'd been surprising when Damon had won her over our senior year in high school. Phoenix and I had secretly been rooting for her, especially after the bullshit her friend had pulled by bullying her.

"I found a house," Cole dropped. "It's big enough for all of us."

"Is it Riley approved?" Phoenix asked. "If it is, then Aspen will be more excited to move in. She doesn't think we'll pick something livable."

I snorted. "Like the usual frat houses?"

"Yep, floors sticky with beer and other things." Phoenix zipped his bag. "That's what she's picturing. She also worries about everyone's sleep getting disrupted because the baby will be less than one by then."

"Shit. It still blows my mind. Out of all of us, I thought I'd be the first with a kid." Secretly, I was glad it wasn't me. I was less ready than my brother.

"Goes to show prior experience with long-term relationships doesn't count for shit."

I couldn't even fuck with my brother on that one. "I guess when you meet the right one, nothing else matters. Aspen is amazing, bro. Don't fuck it up."

"You're fucking things up enough for all of us." Damon's dark-blue eyes glittered. "Get your shit together, and you better let us know when you need us. No more of this I'll-deal-with-it-on-my-own bullshit."

I fucking loved my family. Nothing else needed to be said.

CHAPTER THIRTEEN

WINTER

Monday classes came and went without me in them. It was a bad idea to skip so early in the semester, but I couldn't bring myself to go after last night, when Landon had peppered me with questions about my family. The past had haunted me too much to focus on anything else.

My hands hovered over the keys of my laptop as I stared at a picture of McMillan Lake. The building's name wasn't hard to pull from my memories, but so much was fuzzy. Throat tight with the usual fear that strangled me, I got the address of the Sea Mist Apartments and typed it into my phone's map app. That year would be the beginning of reconciling with the darker times in my life. I glanced to where I'd stashed the shoebox full of Mom's letters and snorted. *Within reason.* That wasn't something I was ready to tackle.

Keys in hand, I headed to my car, ready to face things I hadn't wanted to. I still didn't. But Mom's parole hearing loomed overhead. I needed to understand what had happened and try to figure out the parts I couldn't remember.

The half-hour drive went by in a blur. I followed the GPS until I reached my destination. Parked in front of a run-down apartment building not far from the lake, I turned off the car and took in the scene.

The place was a dump—a brown building with paint peeling on the trim. The front steps were cracked, and the black wrought iron railing had a few broken and rusted spindles. The landscaping was sparse and tired looking. It matched the building perfectly. The only out-of-character spot was one of the balconies. Flowers lined the railing, a burst of color in otherwise drab surroundings—an oddity in Section 8 housing.

I exited my car, shut and locked the door, then leaned against it while staring at the building I'd lived in with my mom and sister after Dad had died and before moving to Los Angeles. Emotions swelled, weighing me down. I had some decent childhood experiences but very few I could remember. The bad ones eclipsed the good.

Another balcony had towels, pants, and shirts draped over the railing. A bright-red kid's toy table and chairs occupied another. Nothing spoke to me from my past. The psychologist said the trauma I'd suffered shielded me and made everything before I moved away fuzzy. She said the repressed memories could come back, or some of them.

The longer I stood there, the more a hazy image surfaced of my sister and me walking up the front steps. We were young. Maybe eight or nine years old. It had to be from when our dad had died. Everything had gone to hell after that.

A year older, Summer had taken the brunt of everything—Mom's rage and helping me in too many ways. But when it came to survival, we did our best to care for each other. We were equal in that—until I'd failed her.

We'd lived on the third floor, one apartment from the flowery balcony. It would do me no good to knock on that door.

Another fortifying breath and I pushed off the car to trudge up the sidewalk to the building's front door. When I turned the handle, it wasn't locked, and I shoved it open. It was dark inside.

Noise leaked beneath the doors and down the stairs. It was mostly quiet, but I could remember when it hadn't been, when people had argued, a dog had barked, and the drone of TVs had filled the hallway. Most people were at work.

Something was there for me. I could feel it. The balcony with the flowers was the second one on the left side. With that information, I climbed the stairs, found the coinciding door, and knocked.

The low murmur of a game show played somewhere inside. I didn't have to wait long before a scuff sounded and the door cracked open, a chain the only thing that barred me from the older woman with a mop of short, curly gray hair, dark eyes, and a pale, papery face peering at me from within.

Thin lips formed an O, and the door shut in my face. A second later, the sound of metal scraped wood, then it opened without the barrier of the chain. "Winter?"

"You know me?" As I said it, images flooded my mind. All of them good and happy with her.

"Of course I do. You're the spitting image of your mama."

My smile froze, but I fought the repulsion of being compared to the woman who had killed my sister. It wasn't Mrs. C's fault, and I pushed through the emotions. "Ah, sorry. I remember. Hi, Mrs. C."

"Oh hush, call me Estelle."

My shoulders dropped an inch as I stepped inside her apartment. It was warm and homey. Worn, flowery furniture with handmade throw pillows and knickknacks filled the space. Lemon permeated the place from the cleaner Estelle liked to use, and it was one of my favorite smells even then. Summer and I had always felt safe there.

But she hadn't always been available to watch us when Mom didn't want us underfoot. Estelle had watched her grandkids at their house on the other side of town a few days a week. A chill danced over my skin despite how overly warm it was in her place. It was one of those days when Mom had dragged Summer and me to the lake.

"Come visit, dear." Mrs. C motioned to the couch.

I sank onto a soft cushion, tugged the throw pillow forward, and hugged it. Nothing had changed inside, and it gave me a level of comfort.

"Do you want anything to drink?"

"No." I smiled, doing my best to appear relaxed. *How could I be with what I needed to ask her?* It was too soon to start, though. I glanced around at the frames that crowded her coffee table. "Wow, your grandbabies have grown."

She picked up one close to her. "Do you remember Johnnie? He's on the baseball team now. This was taken last year. He has one more season before he graduates. And this"—she plucked a blue frame with a little girl in a tutu off the table—"this is Jenni. She's just a darling. You never met her. She's the youngest of the three. Travis is in the one closest to you. Do you remember the boys?"

"A little, but it's been a long time since I've seen you."

She patted my arm then leaned back. "It has. Such a shame what happened to your sister." Her eyes misted. "I'll never forgive myself for not being more involved. If I hadn't gone to Rachel's that day, maybe Summer would still be here."

"Maybe. But I don't think what happened could have been avoided. If not that day, then another. It wasn't the first time Mom took us to the lake."

"She was a sweet little thing." Estelle wiped a tear from the corner of her eye.

That wasn't a path I wanted to go down. "I came today to try to remember some stuff about my mom." Her lips pressed together as she waited for me to say more. "Do you remember where she used to work?"

"Well… your mama didn't work." Estelle glanced away, her fingers pulling at a loose thread on her blouse.

I stilled. I didn't want to read into what Estelle didn't say about how we grew up after Dad died. The way our mom had behaved sometimes and the men that had come and gone at odd hours told me things I didn't want to admit. "Did she sell drugs or something else?" She was a drug addict. That I knew for a fact. The other, I wasn't sure about.

"I don't know about that."

"I remember a lot of men coming in and out of our apartment."

She nodded once.

"Did a man live with her? He had curly blond hair."

Estelle shook her head. "I'm sorry, Winter. To my knowledge, no one lived there but you three. But if someone who fit that description did, I don't remember."

"It's okay. I don't remember either."

I stayed for a half hour and caught Estelle up on what I'd been doing for the last few years. It was the least I could do for everything she had done for me and my sister growing up.

Back in my car, and with a pit of loneliness taking up space in my stomach, I couldn't handle visiting the lake. That could wait for another day.

Before heading back to campus, I checked my phone. It only made me feel worse. Landon hadn't called or messaged me. Not once.

CHAPTER FOURTEEN

SHANE

Things were not going my way. The plan had been to check in with Mom after classes but before she went into the hospital for her shift and ask her if she remembered anything regarding Winter, then I would work out. It didn't happen. She had to work a double and had gone in early. Since I was already on the road when I found out, I changed course to Grandad's.

Just after dinner, traffic wasn't too bad. It was still light out. When I got off the highway, I lowered the windows. It was cooler out, but I was still hot from lifting and would probably need to grab something else to eat later. Maybe Grandad would be up for going out too.

Once there, I let myself in with the key he'd given me years ago. "Grandad?"

I wandered deeper into the house until I heard him yelling. He paused, then more shouting came from the office. The door to his study was open, and I stopped in the entryway. He met my gaze and waved me in.

The sleeves of his dress shirt were rolled and shoved up past his elbows. Rarely did I see him with rumpled clothing, but he was. That alone set me on edge.

"This should be over with." The pen he held went flying. "I pay you good money to make sure everything is taken care of."

I stood near his desk as a bad feeling washed over me. He was always yelling at someone. I couldn't remember when something hadn't set him off, when he'd been happy for an extended period. For someone who had more money than God, but maybe not as much as Uncle Lucas, the old man was a grumpy fuck.

"Fine. But I want it done here, in my office." He slammed the phone down then scrubbed a hand over his face, looking every year of his age at that moment.

The call had been about me. I braced myself to hear whatever he would tell me. From what he'd said, it had to be the attorney on the other line that Grandad had hired to represent me when I was arrested.

"What's going on?"

"There's no easy way to say this, son. Since they filed a civil case, there's a chance that the criminal case could be reopened. It's slight and, I think, a ploy by the Green family. I doubt the DA would reopen it when it's based on the evidence that proved you acted in self-defense."

Goddammit. I fell into the chair in front of his desk, my knees buckling as I felt my future slipping from my grasp. "I don't understand." But I did. Something new had happened.

"Another witness has come forward."

"No one else there had a clear view." After registering the horror of what had happened, I'd visually swept the area. Erica Williams, the girl whose family had hired me to keep her safe, had been the only one, and she would never testify against me.

"I don't have all the details. What I do know is that someone overheard an argument between Luke and you when you were acting as a bodyguard. Luke's family has money, and they're throwing their weight around."

"That kid was a problem. I can't see how the argument made me look bad." I thought back to the discussions I'd had with Luke, telling him to stay the fuck away from Erica. But maybe it didn't matter. The Green family was out for blood, specifically mine. They would find someone who'd heard us and could be swayed to their side. I was sure of it. "What am I supposed to do?"

"The cops want you to come in for an interview. The Green family put pressure on the police for a criminal case, but the attorney assured me that will not happen. It's more of a formality and to get them to come to terms with the decision. They have some pull with the police chief, and you'll be questioned. That's it. You will not be charged or arrested. Regardless, I think the interview should be done here."

I took in the dark-wood bookcases and oversized mahogany desk. Grandad sat behind it like a king on his throne. It was intimidating as hell and not a bad idea. I needed as many things on my side as I could get, but my gut twisted at the thought of trying to control the location. They might see it as the manipulative move it was and put another strike against me.

"No." I held his gaze unflinchingly. "I need to do this—face whatever is coming."

Bushy white eyebrows furrowed as he held my gaze. My jaw ached from how tightly I clenched my teeth. It was the right thing to do, and I wouldn't let him talk me out of it. He must've seen something in my expression because I could tell by the way his shoulders suddenly slumped that he'd decided to back down. Then he stood and reached across the desk, holding his hand to me. I shook it, standing taller at the gleam of respect shining in his eyes.

"I'll go with you."

"No. I need to do this on my own."

His frown cut deep lines around his mouth, but he relented. "I don't like it, but I'll respect your decision." He picked up his phone and hit a few buttons as I turned for the door. "And Shane?" He paused, waiting for me to look his way, phone pressed to his ear. "The lawyer will meet you there."

I nodded then left as Grandad ordered the lawyer to get his ass to the precinct immediately.

I understood the underlying issue. The Greens would file a civil case against me, and they would probably win. Grandad was worried about that too. I could see it in his face.

My hands were clammy as I gripped the steering wheel tightly. When I got to the police station parking lot, I just sat there, my outlook bleak. It wouldn't end well for me. If I'd known what would come of hitting Luke, I never would have done it. A restrained hold would have been easy. *Why the hell did I have to punch him back?*

I rested my forehead against the steering wheel. I knew why I'd done it. He'd swung first. It was instinctual, and I was fed up with how he'd been treating Erica. But goddamn, I never wanted him to die. Just go the fuck away.

Another glance around the parking lot showed that the lawyer hadn't arrived. I would have called Uncle Lucas, but from our last meeting, it'd been established that Grandad's lawyer would keep him in the loop. I waited in the parking lot. No way would I go in without him. With a few minutes to spare, I hit the Contact button to call Mom. If I was going to jail, I wanted her to know I loved her. Asking about Winter was no longer a priority. Not with my shit hanging over my head.

The police chief had asked me three questions, all of which my lawyer had shut down. They had no case, and it was made clear. But Mr. and Mrs. Green had been prepared for that. Good thing Grandad and my lawyer had been as well, and I'd been briefed before entering the room to let him speak for me without contest.

We moved to a conference room. The only ones in attendance were the Greens, myself, and our lawyers. We sat at a conference table, facing each other. I studied them and how their grief clung to them in different ways. Mrs. Green's brown eyes were red rimmed and puffy, her hands shaking so much that her husband gently pressed them under the table and onto her lap. She couldn't meet my eyes. I didn't blame her. I struggled to look in the mirror on occasion as well.

"I'm sorry." The words came out before I could think of the consequences, but they needed to be said. "If I could take back what happened to your son, I would. I never meant any real harm."

Frank's hand pressed on my shoulder—the slight pressure telling me to stop talking. I did. Mrs. Green's head snapped up, her grief blasting me. Something moved in those brown depths. *A slight ease of pain maybe?* I hoped I'd read her right, that my words had helped in some tiny way. It had to mean something that I hadn't wanted, or wished for, her son's death.

"Bullshit," Mr. Green growled. "You'd hit him before. It was with intent. And it's a goddammed travesty the justice system did not prevail—yet. But it will. Mark my words."

"That's enough," their lawyer, Mr. Miller, said.

Frank cleared his throat, and I tore my gaze from Mr. Green's zealous one.

"What are your clients' needs?"

Mrs. Green gasped, but I kept my head down. To have their son back, obviously. *But since that's impossible...*

"We seek mental damages for losing their only son and compensation for Luke's anticipated role in Green Pharmaceuticals."

"My client is confident that if the case went to court, the ruling would be in our favor."

The lawyers shared a pointed look.

"However," my lawyer continued, "my client is willing to settle, but there are stipulations. If they are not agreed to, we will have no choice but to go to trial."

An ache formed in my jaw. I held still, barely breathing as I waited for their lawyer to read over the documents Frank pushed to their side of the table.

"We will need a moment to confer," Mr. Miller said.

Frank and I stood then left the room.

Air whooshed out of me on the other side of the closed door, and I leaned a shoulder against the wall. It was more to keep myself from dropping to the ground than anything. "What do you think will happen?"

"They'll sign." Frank's phone rang. He answered and pressed it to his ear.

The agreement was that the Green family would not seek retribution through slander and could not bring forward any new or fabricated evidence. They were not allowed to speak my or my family's name in relation to what had happened or with ill intent. If they broke any of those sticking points, we would sue for more than the payout they would receive, plus legal fees and punitive damages.

It took ten minutes before the door opened and we were due back in the conference room.

"Mr. and Mrs. Green have agreed," Mr. Miller announced.

"We'll need a witness." Frank stepped out of the room, making sure I went with him.

The next fifteen minutes were a blur as the Greens signed the witnessed documents in duplicate, and with each signature inked, my lungs expanded a little farther. I should have known that feeling of hope wouldn't last.

CHAPTER FIFTEEN

WINTER

I couldn't shake the conversation I'd had with my old neighbor Estelle earlier. And no amount of homework or streaming shows worked. The walls of my dorm room pressed in on me. I'd even called work to see if I could pick up an extra shift, but they were covered.

With nothing to occupy my thoughts, scattered memories pushed through the door in my mind where I'd kept everything locked away of before Mom had gone to jail. What had once been the only coping mechanism my younger self would allow against the pain was riddled with cracks that I knew would one day release everything.

Charcoal smudged my fingers, and torn-off pages from my sketch pad littered my bed, all with the same image—the faceless man from my nightmares.

The door to my room opened, and I jumped.

Piper walked in, her long blond ponytail swinging behind her. Her eyes widened as she took in the mess around me. "Whoa." She came closer, pinched one of the drawings, and studied it briefly. Concern clouded her blue eyes. "What's going on here?"

She released the sketch, and it floated back to rejoin the pile of similar ones on my bed. My cheeks heated. It was weird that the faceless guy sometimes visited my dreams and haunted my mind. And after returning to where I'd lived with my mom and sister, I couldn't exorcise him from my thoughts. That was what happened. Hundreds of faceless images, shrouded in shadows and with a swirl of different backgrounds, plagued me. I couldn't draw fast enough to purge them from my brain.

"I don't know." It was the best answer I could give. "It's something I've seen in my dreams." *More like nightmares.*

"This doesn't look like a good dream." She dropped her bag by the corner of her desk before sitting on her bed and facing me. "Does this have to do with what happened when you were a kid?"

I shrugged. "I…" *Did it?* "I'm not sure. It's someone from my past." I gave up and tossed my sketchbook and charcoal pencil onto the comforter with the rest of the drawings. "I think my mom's parole is bringing up all kinds of stuff that I'd forgotten."

Piper pulled up her legs and sat cross-legged. "That's understandable. It was years ago and very traumatic. I couldn't imagine losing my sister and my mom in the same year, let alone in the same month."

"I just want it to stop, but he keeps reappearing in my mind." I dropped my face into my hands, wishing I could escape all the crap with my mom.

"Have you shown any of those drawings to the police?"

"No, but that isn't a bad idea." I needed to decide on if I would go to Mom's hearing. Maybe they had information on file that could help identify who the man was and how he connected to my family.

Piper swung her legs over the side of the bed, her foot bouncing furiously. "Do you want me to go with you?"

I pressed my lips together, suppressing the surprised laugh.

Her body language clearly said she didn't want to. "No, but thanks. I'm sure it'll be a wasted effort."

Her leg stopped moving. "Well, if it is, at least you tried."

I glanced at the time. It was after dinner, something I'd skipped. "I'm surprised to see you here. You've been gone almost all week after classes." I suspected she had a boyfriend. I didn't usually see her until I woke up the next morning to find her back from a shower and getting ready for morning classes. *Wait, maybe it's me she's avoiding?* "Is it me? Do you not want to room with me because it's weird?"

I'd been living with the loss of my sister for years. I could still see her in the shape of my eyes and the same smile reflected in my pictures and the mirror. Our laughs had sounded very similar. That one didn't slap me in the face as often, as laughing wasn't something I'd done the first year after she'd died. It was only through continued effort on my foster family's part that had eased the ache enough, so I tried to be happy. With them anyway.

Piper pulled the length of her hair forward. It was long enough to fall over her shoulder even though she wore a ponytail. She wound the gold strands around her finger, biting her lower lip for a second. "Okay." Her hand dropped back to her lap. "I'm not gonna lie and say it's easy. When I look at you, I wonder what Summer would be like if she were here. We were close, then she was gone, and you… changed." She held up her hand to stop me from speaking. "I get it. What you were going through was unimaginable, and we were kids. But… I don't know. We've talked, and I'm getting to know you again. So, it's not weird. I was just surprised when I learned you would be my new roommate. I'm glad you're here, Winter. Really, I am. It's just been a bit of an adjustment." She offered a small smile to show she was sincere.

I shoved some of the mess out of the way and hopped off my bed, then hugged her quickly. "Thanks. And thank you for suggesting talking to the police. I think I'll do that now, since I can't stop thinking about"—I waved toward the papers—"whatever this is."

"That's probably a good idea. And I'm in for the night if you need to talk or want to go to the library when you get back."

"Is your boyfriend busy, then?"

Her brows rose. "Y—no." Her eyes narrowed.

That time, I laughed. "You never said anything about dating someone to me. It was a guess."

She huffed a breath. "It's new. I don't want to jinx anything."

"No worries. Tell me about him when you're ready." I grinned then gathered a few sketches and shoved them into my messenger bag. "I'll see you later."

I plugged the police station into my map app as I walked to my car. It wasn't far. Maybe ten minutes away. It was still light out, but not for much longer. Only a few open parking spots remained when I turned into the lot. I found one close to the main entrance then headed inside.

In the front room, I stepped up to the plexiglass divider that went to the ceiling.

The woman in uniform behind the thick layer of protection hung up the phone and gave me her full attention. "How can I help you?"

"Hi, I'm Winter Patten, and I'm hoping to talk to someone about Katrina Patten's upcoming parole hearing. Or whoever would be in charge of her case." I had no idea what I was doing.

She picked up the phone receiver, hit a button, and repeated what I'd asked to whoever was on the other end. "An officer will be with you in one moment."

"Okay. Thanks." I stepped away from the glass and off to the side. Some plastic chairs lined one side of the small waiting room—or foyer. I didn't know what that space was called. All I knew was that I was uncomfortable.

A few minutes later, a loud buzz sounded, and an officer

held open the door. He was about my height with close-cropped salt-and-pepper brown hair and a large nose. "Winter Patten?"

"Yes." I hurried forward and passed through into the station. The sounds of people pounding away on their keyboards, talking on their phones, and the faint crackle of dispatch filled the open area as he guided me into his space.

"I'm Officer Blare." He stopped at a messy desk and waved toward one of the two chairs on the other side. "The private rooms are all full, so we'll have to talk here."

That was my cue. "I was wondering what you could tell me about my mom's case. She's up for parole, and I've been invited to speak, but I can't remember much other than my sister and I being pushed into the lake."

"That would be Detective Jaimeson's territory. Let me see if he's available to speak to you." He pushed up from his chair and went in search of the detective.

I followed him with my gaze, nervous about being in there. He disappeared for a moment. When he came back, not even five feet behind him, another person snagged my attention, and I froze. Landon exited a room down the hall. Two men flanked him, a man in a suit and an officer. The suit spoke to him, and Landon didn't look my way as I waved.

Did he not see me?

He didn't turn my way once. I jumped as Officer Blare retook his seat, his eyes sharp and intense in a way that made me uncomfortable.

"Do you go to Thane University?"

"Yes." *What did that have to do with anything I'd asked?* "Why?"

"What happened at Thane is pretty big news." His dark gaze was unwavering. "Did you know the guy who died?"

"What guy?" His question sparked a memory of Piper telling me about a kid that had died. "Luke Green? I don't know anything. I'd heard about it, but I hardly know anyone from school. I just transferred there." It was weird, and I disliked how the officer looked at me. "Were you able to find the detective in charge of my mom's case?"

"The detective you need to speak to is in with a suspect right now, but I'll get him your name and number. He'll call you when he's free."

"That's okay. I'll just come back another time."

I didn't bother leaving my sketches with the officer to give to the detective. They would be a waste of time. *What could they get from a sketch with no face?*

When I pushed open the heavy door to leave the precinct, Landon was leaning against one of the cement pillars, waiting for me. Some of the day's heaviness lifted when he grinned, and I swore I could've drowned in his smile.

I stepped toward him, and the hair rose on the back of my neck. It was the same eerie feeling I'd been having lately, and I glanced around to see if I could spot whoever was watching me.

"What's wrong?"

I jumped at his voice. Heat flooded my face. *Could I be any more dramatic?* I needed to downplay how weird I was being. "Nothing. I just feel like someone's been watching me. I'm sure it's nothing." I hoped so.

He closed the distance between us, one hand resting on the small of my back, chasing away my nerves. I wanted to lean into him so badly and barely stopped myself from doing it.

"Want to get out of here? Maybe go somewhere alone?"

Yes, please. I had a fleeting thought to ask him to take me to McMillan Lake, but I also didn't want him too close to the crazy in my life. He probably knew about my mother and the case if he was from nearby, but I wouldn't point it out for him if he didn't.

We stood unmoving until I realized he was waiting for me to answer. If it was possible to blush even more, I managed it. Great, not embarrassing at all. I mentally rolled my eyes at myself. "Yeah, I would love to go somewhere else, but my car is here."

"We can come back for it."

"Sounds good." Maybe for a little while, I could just enjoy being my age and pretend like the past wasn't staring me in my face. It was worth a try.

CHAPTER SIXTEEN

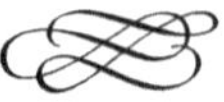

SHANE

The interview had aged me. Stress and exhaustion fairly overwhelmed me. *Then seeing Winter in the police station, talking to that cop? The one who'd been on the scene for Luke's accident when the police first arrived?* Something about it didn't sit right.

"Is everything okay?"

We still stood on the front steps of the cop shop. I needed to get out of there, and since she said she was up for going with me, I guided her to my SUV.

"Yeah, I'm good." I opened the passenger door and waited for her to climb in. "Why were you at the police station?"

"I was there for research." She clicked the seat belt into place. "Why were you there?"

"I had to take care of some speeding tickets." I shut her door then got in on the driver's side. I needed to get away from Thane for a while, and after pulling out of the parking lot, I pointed us toward the cove.

A silence stretched between us that the low drone of music from my speakers failed to disguise.

"You're sure everything's okay?" She angled more toward me in her seat, pulling her hair over one shoulder. "You look tired. If you need to talk, I'm a good listener."

I didn't say anything for the entire ride. Instead, I weighed my options. I wasn't a bad person, not entirely. And I felt like an asshole for lying—even to her.

As I turned into the state park, several tall cliffs and a cove appeared. The water rippled, sparkling from the last rays of the sun. It was deep enough to dive from several rocky ridges that soared overhead.

After I parked and we got out, I took her hand and led her to the small patch of sand at the entrance to the water. "We used to come here all the time in high school." Something she would have known if she'd stayed. But she hadn't, so I was giving her a peek into my past. "My cousin's girlfriend used to dive here whenever possible. Aspen, too, but not from the highest point."

Winter tilted her head back and peered at the precipice. "From up there?"

I laughed because Riley was brave. "Not always from that high, but she jumped from there enough to give the rest of us heart attacks." I sat on the rough sand and pulled Winter between my legs so her back was against my chest.

"I can't even imagine doing that or being okay with anyone else risking their life like that."

"She's an Olympic hopeful, though. The girl has crazy skills."

"Still… that looks like sudden death." She shivered.

"Are you cold?" It was chilly, but I didn't think it was enough to cause the tremor that ran through her.

"No. Just not a fan of water."

I rested my chin on top of her head, breathing in the scent of spiced apples from her hair. She felt so good in my arms, and I wanted to focus on that rather than focusing on her fears, for the time being, anyway. "My dad abandoned my mom when she was pregnant. My brother and I never had contact with him, nor did we want to. But it left scars, not having a dad around, knowing that we didn't matter. He reached out this year and wanted to reconnect."

Winter twisted in my arms enough to read my expression. I braced for something cruel from her but found only concern.

"Did he explain why he left?"

I recalled confronting him and the proof he'd shown me. "He blamed it on my grandad. Even showed me the uncashed check from Grandad to get the hell out of our lives."

"Oh." Her mouth formed an O. "Why did your grandad want him away from your family?"

"He did some things when he was younger that my grandad found out about. Something dangerous. Joe—my dad—claims it was self-defense. It's hard to know who to believe. People lie." That last part I made a point about on purpose.

Her hand settled on my forearm, and the heat from her touch seared me. "Sometimes, they don't lie. And sometimes, they don't have any other choice but to. You should go with your gut on this."

"Joe asked me to go into business with him." I left out anything that had to do with my brother. That was on a need-to-know basis, and I was already going out on a limb letting her in a little. I shouldn't, but something about her made me want to trust her. It was stupid, and yet, I couldn't resist.

"Do you want to do that?"

"Go into business with him?"

She nodded, and I snorted. "I shouldn't. It's not smart, but I want to give him a chance. I respect my grandad. He was there for us every day, no matter what. But if Joe is telling the truth"— and I suspected he was, based on the bullshit Grandad had tried to pull with Aspen—"everything changes."

Winter shifted, and I loosened my arms so she could turn and face me. Her hands slid up my arms, over my shoulders, then tangled in the back of my hair. Her touch soothed me and made me want to grab her and pull her beneath me.

When we were younger, I'd thought she was so pretty with her strawberry-blond hair and a smile that had made my stomach do backflips. And she was, on the outside. But darkness had swirled when I'd looked into those grass-green eyes with gold around her pupils. It should have warned me off, the glimpse into the cruelty of her soul.

I found none of that when I looked at her now. Kindness, concern, and a hint of longing were crystal clear. *Can I trust myself in this?* She listened, and it didn't seem like she was judging me. My mind wouldn't let go of the fact that she was the same person who had made me want to end it all.

I should hate her. My grandad would want me to. I couldn't. I didn't understand why. I wanted to hate her, to punish her. But the way she looked at me, how she felt in my arms, and when she touched me told me she wasn't the same person.

I dropped my gaze to her full lips. Her fingers tightened in my hair, and when I met her eyes, what I saw told me she wanted me as much as I wanted her.

My hands found her waist, and I lifted her so her legs settled on either side of mine. Then I pulled her closer, moving slowly so she had time to pull back if she didn't want it. I kept my touch light as I brushed my lips against hers. I had no reason to rush, and I kept a tight rein on my control.

Then I grazed her bottom lip with my teeth, and a shudder ripped through her. It was the response I needed, and I slanted my mouth over hers, pulling her close. I took my time exploring. Her tongue tangled with mine, urging me to deepen the kiss. I rose to the challenge, sliding my hand up her back until I had a grip on the hair at her nape. I angled her head, teasing her until she moaned and pressed impossibly closer. She tasted as amazing as she had during our first kiss.

It was easy to get lost in the feel of her, in the way she

responded in my arms. On that thought, I slowed the kiss before breaking it. Our breaths crashed against each other's. Goddamn, she was going to be a problem. The kiss hadn't been part of my plan but rather because she'd listened to me. And maybe because she'd outgrown being an asshole.

I lifted her off me until she was seated next to me. Water softly lapped at the edge of the shore, and the light leached from the sky as the sun descended. It was time to head back to Thane and reality. Soon. I wasn't quite ready to break the spell of our time together.

"Who are you, Landon? I know almost nothing about you."

"Just someone who's interested in you." I was curious about hearing things from her point of view, as opposed to what I'd read online. "What was your childhood like?"

She stiffened beside me, but I didn't turn my head to see her expression. Instead, I gave her time to break down her walls and let me in, as I had with her.

"It was pretty basic."

I fought my reaction. *Bullshit.* Nothing about her childhood was basic. Everything we'd built between us imploded. She was a fucking liar.

"Hey, the cop asked me if I knew anything about the guy who died."

I just bet he did. And the fact that she'd kissed the person responsible had to be of interest to the police.

"I thought it seemed weird. Did they ask you about it too?"

Instead of answering her, I got to my feet and held out my hand to her. "We should get back. I'll drop you at your car."

Her brows furrowed, and I wanted to cup her face and kiss her again, despite her lying mouth. My mind warred against my body, but it was one battle I was determined to control. I walked beside her, holding her hand and pretending I didn't hate her with every fiber of my being.

We were in the car when my phone rang and Phoenix's name flashed across the screen. I answered immediately. "Hey, what's up?"

"Aspen's having contractions. I'm taking her to the hospital."

CHAPTER SEVENTEEN

WINTER

They were there, taunting me—Mom's letters. I could feel them under my bed. I'd only agreed to bring them with me because coming to Thane was about facing my past and moving on. That was what Brooke and I had talked about and had decided with my therapist. I was on board, just struggling.

Brooke and James had originally wanted me to open them at their house so I would have support. I wasn't ready. So my plan was a compromise of sorts, and after my ineffective visit to the police station, it was time.

The room was quiet. Piper had texted that she would be staying with her boyfriend that night but to message if I wanted to get together for dinner or anything. Not after my day. Spending time with Landon had been the exception. Otherwise, too much pressed on me. The run-down apartment building where I'd lived with my mom and sister, talking with Estelle, then that creepy feeling like someone was watching me. It'd been happening more often, and I wasn't sure if it was real or just the past crowding closer.

Piper's side of the room was a constant reminder of my sister. She'd loved pink, and I'd associated the color with her for so long. It served as another reminder that I needed to face her death and not through the eyes of a child. Something was missing, and I'd felt that for a long time. I had to face the letters from Mom. It was the most logical place to jump-start my memories.

I dragged the shoebox along the floor, out from the shadows, and dropped it onto my bed, where I climbed on after it. I got comfortable with pillows behind my back then flipped open the lid. Bundled in stacks of twelve each, I decided to start with the oldest letter and work my way to the most recent. I lost time in the ramblings of my half-crazed mother's messy scrawl.

Daughter,

Why didn't you listen? I told you ungrateful girls to stay out of trouble. But you didn't. And look what happened? You were the worst of the two of you. Always being difficult. It's all your fault. Everything.

Mom didn't bother to sign that one. Or any of the ones that rambled and accused me, without even saying my name, of everything that had gone horribly wrong.

Spawn,

You're a fool. Do you think what happened to your sister won't happen to you? It's not me you need to worry about. You'll get yours. I wish you were never born.

I wanted to throw up. That was the mother I remembered, high on drugs or falling all the way down and desperate for more. She'd hurt us then in so many ways. With words, with kicking us out, and sometimes she'd even hit us. Summer had taken the brunt of it. She always did. Tears rolled down my face, and I battled the waves of nausea as I pressed on. I would get through them, and it would hopefully be my last time. If I was honest, I never wanted them to let her out. She could rot in there, and it still wouldn't be enough.

I tensed as I was catapulted into the past just from Mom's vile words. Summer and I were young. I was maybe nine years old, and we huddled in a corner of our closet. We shared a room in the two-bedroom apartment where we lived.

Others had come into the living room with Mom. We could hear them, and it sent paralyzing fear into us both. I pressed into my sister's side, our hands gripped tightly between us. She was my lifeline.

I was so hungry, and I knew she was too. When my stomach growled, it set hers off. If Mom and the others weren't out there, we could sneak into the kitchen to look for food. If we couldn't find any, we sometimes went to Mrs. C's. She always shared.

But we couldn't leave the closet. We even had a small bucket because the bathroom wasn't an option either. *If they found us...*

I shook myself violently and withdrew from the memory. Fucking drug addicts. I hated everything to do with substance abuse. Bitterness coated my tongue. My sister and I had been terrified when Mom had thrown her parties. She was no mother to us, not after Dad had died.

As I read on, finishing the first year she was sent to jail, her lunatic ramblings and threats changed. She seemed almost normal. Or as close to it as I could imagine she knew how to be. And that I trusted even less than the letters her first year.

Winter,

I don't blame you. What happened was horrible. I've cried so many tears for Summer. I wish it had been me who died, never her. She looked so much like her father. Things were better when he was alive. We were happy. I know you won't understand this, but his death shook me. I had no income. And your father didn't have life insurance. I was left with debt and two little girls to raise.

We hadn't planned to get pregnant. Since being incarcerated, I've learned that I have some issues that need deep counseling. I'm addressing that, my darling daughter. I'm better, and I'll keep at it to make sure I never get that low again.

But most of all, I want you to know that I'll never let anyone hurt you, like what happened to your sister. I'll always protect you.

Love,

Mom

Bullshit. I felt sick. *How dare she? Protect me? Like she wished she'd done for Summer? Against who—herself?* She was just as crazy as always but worse because she thought she'd gotten the help she needed. It was self-righteous crap and a way to absolve herself of what she'd done.

I would never forgive her for taking my sister from me. When I finished reading as much as I could, I had a blinding headache and no more answers than when I'd started. I reordered and bound the letters before putting them back into the box. Worthless, every last one of them. I glanced at the time. It was ten thirty and late, but I needed to talk to Brooke. I pulled up her name, hit the button to connect the call, then waited.

"Winter? Is everything all right?" Concern laced her voice, giving me the anchor I needed.

"Sort of." A beep sounded on my end. "Hold on a sec." I pulled the phone from my ear and swiped the screen to read the text.

It was Landon, finally responding to my message asking how his sister-in-law was doing.

> Landon: It's possibly a false alarm but waiting to chat with the doc.
>
> Me: Thanks for the update.
>
> Landon: Hey—thanks for listening to me today. I'm here if you want to talk too.
>
> Me: You can come over after if you want or if you need to talk more.
>
> Landon: Not sure how late I'll be. I'll message you.

I exited the messages and returned to my call, oddly disappointed that he wasn't coming to my room. I didn't want to be alone, and when I was with him, I felt safe—which wasn't normal. The only people I felt safe around were my new family.

"Sorry about that, Brooke. I'm seeing this guy, and he texted."

"Oooh, tell me about him."

I laughed, picturing her infectious grin and how she would snuggle into the corner of the couch. She always had time for Jax and me. It was one of the things I loved so much about her. "I will, but I called about something else."

"I don't like the tone of your voice. Do you need me to drive over there? I will. Jammies and all, you know I don't care."

"No, you don't need to do that." I pulled my knees to my chest and rested my cheek on them. "I just want to talk."

"Okay. I'm here."

"I read most of the letters."

"Oh, damn—I mean shoot, sorry for my French. They had to be heavy. You sure you don't want me to drive over?"

I grinned. "It's okay. I'm good."

Brooke always apologized when she swore unless she was angry at one of us. That didn't happen often and usually only with Jax, because he tested his parents sometimes.

"Did they help?"

"No. She was unhinged that first year. I'm sure she was going through withdrawals." That had absolutely been the case. Mom had been a drug addict, and to quit cold turkey, I was just glad I wasn't around to witness it.

"She got the help she needed. I'm sure it was tough to read them, though."

"Not those, no. It brought back what it was like living with her. Summer and I never knew which side we would get. She would waver from being chill and high to having violent rages." I wished Summer had survived and had lived with Brooke, James, and Jaxon. She would have loved every second of it even more than I had. It tore me up more than I let on to my foster family. But I suspected they knew. I'd opened up some about my sister. She hadn't been perfect, but she'd been mine.

"What did the other letters say?" Brooke asked.

"They didn't make sense, though they were more coherent. She named people I don't know and told me she would always protect me." That made me furious. I'd balled that note up and tossed it into the box as soon as I'd read it. "It's not real. She never protected us."

"I'm sorry, Winter. I'd hoped you would find answers or closure at the very least."

"I know." She and my therapist had meant well. "You have helped me more than my mother could ever pretend to."

"I'm going to come by."

"No, really. I'm okay. I just wanted to talk some of it out with you. I'm going to go to sleep."

"I don't like this. I should be there. Maybe James and I should cancel our vacation."

That was the thing about my foster family. They always supported me. "Ahh—no. This is the first time you guys are going away without me and Jaxon. And it's Hawaii. You cannot cancel. Besides, you are helping by being on the phone with me. I promise I'm fine, just tired." And if they cancelled, Jaxon would call off meeting Max's parents. That was coming up also and was a big deal. I was not screwing with either of those huge events.

"Are you still drawing that—"

"Yeah." I didn't want to revisit the faceless man. "I went to the police station to see if they could somehow place him in relation to my mom's case. The detective wasn't in, but I may try to get ahold of him another time."

"That's a smart idea."

"We'll see." I didn't have high hopes that it would result in anything. "Thanks, Brooke. I love you."

"I love you, too, Winter. Please call me anytime you need me."

"I will."

We said our goodbyes, and I tossed my phone on my bed. After I put the letters away, I felt better. They were out of sight. What I wanted more than anything was to fall asleep in Landon's arms and forget about everything I'd just read, because my mother would never take responsibility for Summer's death.

CHAPTER EIGHTEEN

SHANE

Unease sat heavy in my gut as Phoenix paced the hospital room like a caged animal. I'd never seen him so shaken.

"Hey." Aspen drew Phoenix's attention. "Everything'll be fine."

But she was pale, and I wasn't so sure. They'd thought the baby was coming early. Not due until March, their little girl would have been born a month and a half too soon.

The nurse came back in and checked the monitor. She adjusted the strap around Aspen's stomach. It fed data to the screen, keeping track of her contractions. "The doctor will be in shortly." She patted Aspen's arm.

"Thanks," Aspen said as my phone rang.

Mom's name flashed across the screen. We'd gone to the hospital closest to campus rather than where she worked.

"Hey, Mom."

"Phoenix isn't answering his phone."

Because my brother has lost his mind. I couldn't blame him, though. I doubted I would've reacted differently if the situation were reversed.

"What's going on?" Mom prompted.

"We're waiting on the doc, but Aspen's having some contractions."

"How close are they?"

"Aah. I think ten minutes?" I looked to Phoenix, who nodded. "They're not regular, though. That's the only thing the nurse said."

"Okay, good. Put me on speaker."

I pulled the phone from my ear and hit the button. "You're on speaker now, Mom."

Phoenix whirled, his body so tense I swore I could see the air vibrating.

"If the contractions aren't regular, it's probably a false alarm and Braxton-Hicks contractions. If Aspen is in actual labor, they can give her a shot to stop it."

"Thank you." Some of the worry melted from Aspen's face, and she released her death grip on one of her blond braids. "I wish you were here, Cece. We were worried and didn't know if we should drive to the other hospital."

Mom loved Aspen. We all did. Damon, Cole, Riley, and Sky were on their way. I'd had to come immediately because I felt what Phoenix did. I was on edge, too, but trying to hold it together for my brother.

A code call sounded in the phone's background along with some rustling. "I've got to go, but keep me informed. Everything will be okay. Love you all." Mom disconnected.

Phoenix went to Aspen's side and took her hand in his. I felt like I could take my first full breath. We'd needed that, them especially. And I knew they were kicking themselves for not driving to the hospital where Mom worked in the ER, but at least she could call and check in.

The doc walked in, and I stood.

"I'll wait outside." I didn't stay for them to acknowledge me. I knew the doc would do an exam, and I doubted my brother or Aspen wanted me there when he did. I grinned when I got to the waiting room and found Cole and Riley there with Damon and Sky. "Hey."

"What's going on?" Riley jumped from her seat, Sky not far behind.

I fell into a seat by my cousins. "The doc's with her. I don't know much, but Mom thinks she'll be fine."

Riley sat beside Cole again, and he drew her close to his side with an arm draped around her shoulders. Damon grabbed Sky's hips and pulled her onto his lap, where she snuggled into him.

It wasn't long before Phoenix appeared. "Aspen's fine. Baby's fine." He had dark circles under his eyes.

Questions exploded from us. "What happened?" "Does the doc think the baby will come early?" "How's Aspen?"

Phoenix dropped into a seat and leaned forward, his elbows on his knees. "It was a false alarm. Aspen is doing too much. Lifting things—surfboards—that she shouldn't be."

"Why is she doing that?"

Max was usually there when she worked, or Phoenix set things up for her.

"She's stubborn." He shrugged.

"What does this mean?" Riley twisted her long chestnut hair over her shoulder.

"We need to step up." Sky shifted on Damon's lap so she was facing us.

"Yeah, if I'm not with her, or Max, I need someone else there helping her. She refuses to slow down."

"But she does get that she needs to take it easy, right?" Cole asked.

"Yeah." Phoenix ran his fingers through his hair. "She just wants to keep up with orders for the business, or she gets inspired and doesn't want to wait for me to come back from watching film or whatever I'm doing for football."

"I've got the easiest schedule without sports. I can be there when you guys aren't," Sky offered.

"We'll communicate in the chat so someone is always at your place," Riley decided. "That means you have to tell us when you won't be home, too, Phoenix."

"I will. And thanks." He stood, relief evident in his tired grin. "I'm going to head back to the room. She's being released soon. You guys don't need to wait, but I'll tell her you came."

A few minutes passed as we talked about the week and who would be with Aspen when. The times and names were updated in our group chat, then we disbursed.

I was wired when I got into my SUV. I wanted to meet my niece but not at that early date, when her lungs could be compromised. Too much was happening, and I knew I couldn't sleep. On the off chance that Winter was awake, I messaged her. Her response was immediate.

Winter: *I'm up. Can't sleep.*

Me: *Can I come over? Or is your roommate sleeping?*

Winter: *No, I mean, yes. Piper's not here. Come over. Let me know when you're outside, and I'll come down and let you in.*

Is it smart? No. I shouldn't trust her. I knew she was a liar. But the kicker was that I was lying too.

For one night, I didn't want to think about any of that. I just wanted her.

The drive was quick, and after parking in her dorm's lot, I messaged her that I was there. I glanced up briefly as I walked to the main door. No stars shone in the sky. Thick clouds obscured them and the moon. A storm was coming, and that fit my mood perfectly. Between my worry for Aspen and my whole shit show with the police and lawyers, I was in a dark place.

The unusual strawberry-blond strands caught my eye in the dimly lit lobby. Goddamn, she was beautiful. Her hair fell in soft waves around her face and over her shoulders to a few inches above her narrow waist. I knew from experience it was as silky as it appeared. When she opened the door, a small smile curved her full, begging-to-be-kissed lips. Up close, the storm in her catlike green eyes told me her night had been as rough as mine.

"Hey." She held up two sodas and bags of chips. "I grabbed some snacks. I thought we could watch a movie or talk or whatever."

I took the cans from her and threaded my fingers with hers, then we walked to the stairs and up to the third floor and her room. She confused me because she was so different from the girl I remembered. Dressed in dark-blue pajama pants with little silver stars and a navy cami, she was adorable. It didn't matter what she wore. She was beyond gorgeous, and I was completely captivated by her.

She unlocked her door, and I followed her inside, my gaze lingering on her perfect ass. When she grabbed her laptop, I took it from her and put it back on her desk.

"I don't want to watch a movie."

"Okay." She set the snacks on her desk then climbed onto her bed and crossed her legs, leaving me enough room to sit with her.

I took in her room, not surprised that Piper's side was overly girly. I knew from Cole and Riley that Piper had changed and had finally let go of her dream to marry him. If she had been there, I would've picked Winter up and brought her to my room. I probably should've, but I wanted an extra glimpse into who she was by being among her things.

Her fingers toyed with the hem of her cami as I sat on the bed, entirely too aware of her. I didn't want to talk, but I let her set the tone for what would happen next. I knew what I wanted, and I wasn't sure how long I could hold out before I kissed her. And I wouldn't stop there. I needed to lose myself in all of her.

A cool breeze rushed into the room from the open window, helping cool the heat inside me.

"How long have you lived here?" Winter asked.

I rested my back against the wall. I guessed we were talking. "All my life. I went to Hidden Valley Academy, and before that, I was at Westin." It was the public school that we'd both attended —or for her, at least up to a point.

"I know I went to Westin, too, but I had an accident when I was younger, so I don't remember much about it."

My focus snapped to attention. *Is she finally being honest with me?* "What kind of accident?"

Lightning strobed outside. Three seconds later, a loud clap of thunder followed. It felt like some kind of omen. Electricity charged the air, permeating her room. It wasn't until the rain started to patter that she reached over and slid the window closed—not a moment too soon as the rain beat against the panes. Tension built outside and in as I waited for her response.

"I almost drowned in McMillan Lake." Some color leached from her face.

I pulled her close, my arm around her shoulders. "I'm glad you didn't."

Shock and confusion warred inside me as I realized that I'd meant what I'd said. I'd already known about her almost drowning, but I'd wanted to see if she would tell me. There was more to the story, but I could understand why she wouldn't want to share. If something had happened to my brother, I would have torn the world down.

Part of me still wanted to make her pay. The other half wanted to kiss her until I forgot everything. It was the latter part of me that won.

With one hand, I threaded my fingers through her hair, cupping the back of her head as I angled it then slanted my mouth over hers. She melted into me, her lips parting on a gasp, and I deepened the kiss.

I gripped her waist and lifted her onto me, her legs automatically settling on either side of me. Then I took her lips in a desperate kiss, devouring them, ruthlessly invading her mouth until she moaned.

***

Winter

Landon's mouth was on mine before I had time to process how I'd told him a little about that day at McMillan Lake. Hands in my hair, he tilted my head for that perfect angle as his tongue swept in to tease and possess. It was the most all-consuming kiss I'd ever had, and my head swam from the sensations, my body pliant against the strength of his will.

I moaned, and he swallowed the sound before breaking the kiss as suddenly as he had initiated it. I gasped at the loss. Dilated dark-blue eyes bored into mine, and my breath crashed into his as I struggled for control. Then his hands slid to my waist, and he hovered at the hem of my shirt.

Landon's fingers twitched, but he held still, waiting for something. "I want you."

No words would come, my throat thick with desire. I nodded. With excruciating slowness, he eased my shirt up and over my head. I shivered at the rush of chilly air against my skin. I wore nothing underneath, and he groaned as he saw my breasts. I was inexplicably turned on.

His corded muscles flexed as he pulled me close, and I grasped his wide shoulders. Then he slid his hand up my body and over my stomach to cup one breast. I trembled as nerve endings flared to life at his gentle touch. Threading my hands through his hair, I arched into him as he gently squeezed my breast. He trailed kisses down my neck then took the stiff peak of my nipple into his mouth and sucked. I sighed as waves of desire swept through me, and I shifted uncomfortably, wanting so much more.

His moan vibrated against my skin, and he pulled me more firmly against his body. So very close to what I wanted most, but we had far too many layers between us. I felt almost vulnerable with my shirt off and him fully clothed. That didn't stop him as he slid a hand beneath the waistband of my pajama pants and slid his fingers between my legs to tease my clit. I jerked against him as he then dipped inside. He knew how to touch and tease me to the point that it was too much, and my body squeezed around him.

I was lost in how he controlled my body, and I squirmed against him, trying to get closer. His mouth left my breast, and his gaze locked on mine. The raw hunger in his eyes stole my breath. As he added a second finger, thrusting deep and curling them, I whimpered against the building sensations.

My fingers curled around the hem of his shirt, and I pulled upward. I wanted to feel his skin, to touch and drive him as wild as he drove me. "Take this off. I want to see you," I rasped.

Then his hand was gone from between my legs, and I cried out at the emptiness. A smirk covered his lips, and I took control, grazing my teeth over his bottom one then following it with my tongue to ease the sting. He growled, and I knew he would be on me, so I pulled back.

"Clothes." I wanted them off.

Strong hands gripped my hips, and he lifted me off him with ease, stood, then pulled his T-shirt off. His jeans and boxers were next, and I sucked in a breath at his size. Long and thick, he would feel amazing inside me, and another wave of heat swept through my core. Wetness saturated my panties, and I didn't even care that he would feel it. Maybe he would move faster. Waiting for him to touch me again was excruciating.

I motioned to Piper's desk. "In that dish in the corner, there're condoms."

His brows rose. "Should I ask?"

"They're Piper's, but she'll share."

He grabbed a condom then tossed the wrapper to the floor with the rest of his clothes. His hair was mussed from having my fingers in it, and he looked sexier than I'd ever seen him. I shifted, desperate to run my hands over his sculpted body. He wasn't having it, though.

He leaned over me, one arm encircling my waist, and brought me close. Then he hooked a finger in the waistband of my pajama pants and panties. He inched them down way too slowly, a knowing grin curving his mouth as I urged him to go faster. The trail of his fingers over my bare skin heightened my awareness and had me craving all sorts of wicked things. One final tug and he yanked them free of my body. Then his weight was over mine.

I ran my hands over his chest, exploring how his muscles bulged and dipped beneath my touch. His biceps flexed as he held himself on top of me. I could feel his length against my thigh, and I wanted to shift to bring him closer, but he held me in place.

There was so much I wanted to do, but I gave in to how he made me feel and his control over my body. He knew where to touch, and I buried my hands in his hair as he pressed open-mouthed kisses along my neck to my shoulder. His teeth sank into the sensitive area between my neck and shoulder, driving me wild.

My core throbbed, and I squirmed beneath him, not above begging to get what I wanted. "Landon, please."

He chuckled against my skin, and when he lifted his head, raw hunger stared back at me. Knowing how I affected him and how much he wanted me was powerful and heady.

Then we were skin to skin, and I wrapped my legs around his waist as he pressed against my entrance. A moan escaped my lips as he pushed inside, the sound ending with a gasp as he thrust deep. I lost myself to the feel of him as he pounded into me. I met his every move.

Gripping his back, I loved the feel of his strength beneath my fingers and was greedy for more. He was insatiable as he moved over me and in me. My stomach clenched hard, desire pooling low in my gut. I gasped when he slid a hand down my stomach to dip between my folds and brush against my swollen clit. It didn't take long until I tightened around him. I cried out from the sensations exploding inside me. His mouth covered mine, swallowing how I screamed his name as I came.

He thrust harder, deeper, his moan vibrating against my skin. It didn't take long until he followed my climax with his own. Then he collapsed on top of me, his body heavy and welcoming on mine.

When he grew too heavy, I pushed at his chest, and he rolled to his side, taking me with him. We lay there for a few minutes, catching our breath before he got up to dispose of the condom. I followed, using the bathroom when he left it. Then I was back in bed and his arms, my head resting on his chest while his fingers trailed soothing circles on my back.

We said no words. They weren't needed. My body and mind were languid and content. I tangled my legs with his, and it wasn't long before I fell into a deep sleep.

CHAPTER NINETEEN

WINTER

One side of my body was insanely overheated. I peeled my eyelids open in confusion. Everything from last night rushed back. *I had sex with Landon.* My heart raced. *Whoa. I can't believe I did that.*

Pressed against his hard, muscular chest, I didn't dare move. I wasn't ready to face him—the things we'd done. How I'd fallen apart in his arms. I bit back a moan, my body softening and preparing for him all over again at the mere memory of last night.

I tilted my head back to see his face. Dark stubble shadowed his strong jaw and those eyelashes—I wished mine were as dark and long as his. He was peaceful and looked like he needed to sleep for a month, so I lazily studied him. I wanted to trace my finger over his high cheekbones, the slight crook in his nose that hinted at a former break or two, and his firm lips that made me melt with the memory of them all over my body.

He had one muscular arm thrown over my waist. *Did he hold me throughout the night?* I didn't know why I was freaking out. I had a hot guy in my bed and a memory that even then made me want to wake him and do it all over again. I should be doing that. Instead, I eased away like a wet noodle as I slowly rolled myself out of bed. Once free, I waited to see if he woke. When his chest continued to move at the same slow, steady pace, I tiptoed to the bathroom Piper and I shared with our suitemates.

I took my time brushing my teeth then secured my hair on top of my head so it didn't get wet when I rinsed off in the shower. As I lathered soap in my hands, my mind spun. It wasn't like I was a virgin. I'd lost my v-card in high school to a boy just as inexperienced as I was. But with Landon, we were on another level—it scared the shit out of me.

I shut off the water and toweled dry before putting on lotion and panties. *Maybe he'll be gone when I go back to my room.* I eased the door open and peeked around it. He was still asleep. Part of me was thrilled, and that was what I decided to go with as I carefully climbed back into bed with him.

He threw off heat like my own personal heater, and soon, I drifted back to sleep snuggled against him.

It wasn't until my alarm went off that I stirred awake. Sunlight streamed through my room and glowed behind my closed eyelids. I slowly blinked, realizing I must have fallen asleep for another hour. My hand flattened against the still-warm sheet where Landon had been. He must have woken after I'd passed out for the second time. We both had classes, so I assumed that was where he'd gone.

I couldn't stop the grin as I stretched before flinging off the covers and sliding my feet over the edge. It was uncharacteristic of me, but I wanted to know what we were, not that we had to put a label on it. Friends seemed realistic, at least. *But are we more?* I had no idea. I didn't want to have a boyfriend when I lived with my foster family. *Do I now?* I kind of did.

I pulled clothes out of my dresser, accidentally kicking something. A wallet was on the floor by my bed. It had to be Landon's. Curiosity always beat my good sense, so I opened it and checked his driver's license.

His picture stared back at me, and… *What the fuck?* His name wasn't Landon. It was Shane Bennett. A long-forgotten memory fell into the forefront of my mind, one where I'd said, "St-St-Stupid Stuttering Shane." The memory was foggy, but I distinctly recalled Stuttering Shane.

Why would he lie about who he was to me? Why call himself Landon? The image of the boy—*Shane*—flashed again through my mind, unlocking a part of me I didn't want to face.

Aah. I bent in half, the images from that year coming too fast but slow enough that I experienced them in fractured detail—so much pain.

I slammed mental walls up to keep the lake house out. The fear was a black vortex waiting to suck me in. I wanted to remember but not like that. I didn't think I could take it, and my mind agreed. But fifth grade, the time after the lake house, had already slipped through the cracks.

Shane. I had been drawn to him, even at that age. Despite his strength, I'd sensed a vulnerability that had called to me. But instead of seeking friendship and solace, I'd lashed out viciously.

I dropped to my knees. The pain of losing my sister, of living with our grandparents, who had never wanted us and had barely wanted our mom, expanded inside me as if I were back there. My hands dug into my legs, helpless against the tiny and unhappy house I had been placed in after Summer and my mom were gone.

My grandparents were there. It wasn't their old and brittle bodies that did anything to me but their whiplash words.

"Don't get too comfortable, Winter. You're here now but not for long," Grandma snapped.

I said nothing—my first impression of Mom's parents was terrifying. I couldn't escape to Mrs. C's apartment, where she would feed me and my sister.

There was laughter with her, happiness, and a space where

we weren't on guard, afraid we might say the wrong thing or do something that set off our mom's moods. Or worse, whoever she had over.

My stomach growled loudly.

"We don't have enough for an ungrateful brat," Grandpa huffed, his gnarled and bony finger pointing to a corner in the three-room house, where a pillow and blanket were tossed. "You sleep there."

That had been my welcome to their home. It was temporary. I'd known it would be, but while there, I took all my pain and fear out on the boy who wanted to talk to me at school.

"W-W-Winter." He towered over me, a tension around his mouth whenever he spoke.

Something ugly and dark exploded inside of me. I wanted to hurt someone as much as I was hurting. I narrowed my eyes and stepped closer to the boy with the pretty blue eyes. "St-St-Stupid Stuttering Shane."

He fell back a step, grunting his response. And when he turned, my hand shot out, my fingers curling around his arm, nails digging deep.

"W-W-What do you want?"

I felt people closing in around us. I knew who they were—not his brother or his cousins. He'd come to me. I stayed with the other mean kids. It was what I knew most. I could predict how they would respond, the outcasts. They were like vultures, sweeping in when the wounded one fell, and I was about to deliver the first cut.

"You shouldn't even try to talk, St-St-Stupid Stuttering Shane."

Someone laughed behind me—the nickname I'd given him taking shape on its own.

"You're an idiot. Go away. No one wants you around."

He squared his shoulders, rallying, but I wasn't done. The cruelty that had been spewed at me for the years since Dad died poured from my mouth, desperately needing an outlet. I didn't want to go down alone. I wanted someone else to suffer with me—he with his packed-full lunches his mom made for him. Sometimes they even had a note. I'd read one when it had fallen on the floor—*I'm so proud of you! Have a great day, Shane. Love, Mom.*

The last time someone had said they loved me was when Dad was alive. Mom didn't even like me. Summer had been her favorite, if she was even capable of genuinely caring. She'd never wanted kids. It was something she'd told us often.

"You're defective. Broken," I said to Shane. "Your mom already has a perfect kid. Do everyone a favor, and just go away. No one wants you around."

I gasped, shoving the memory away as fast as it invaded my mind. God, I'd been such a monster. I hadn't stopped there. I'd found him, sought him out. I'd whispered things for only him to hear. Horrible things. And not once had he retaliated or hurt me back. He had known what lived inside me. I could see it when he'd looked at me, and it had only made me lash out harder.

The wallet lay open before me, exposing his driver's license, which had kicked everything off. I grabbed the soft black leather to close it when something white poked out of the billfold portion. I opened it wide and withdrew the folded piece of paper. A part of me was terrified it would be one of the threatening notes left in my mailbox, but when I unfolded it, I learned how very wrong I'd been to think that.

The paper was aged, as it should be, since the first few handwritten lines made it clear Shane had penned it back in elementary school.

I can't talk—Winter's right. I'm stupid. St-St-

Stupid Stuttering Shane. That's what she calls me. I hate it. I can't make my mouth form the words the right way. I don't want to die, but I don't know how to keep going. I'm defective. Broken.

She can see inside me. She knows, even if you don't see everything wrong with me. Or how alone I am. Not good enough.

I'm sorry, Mom. I don't know how to tell you goodbye. You work hard, and paying for the speech lady to help me isn't fair. Phoenix will be here. It'll be better that way. I just want the pain to stop. Please forgive me.

The piece of paper fluttered to the floor, covering Shane's wallet. Tears rolled down my face, blurring everything around me. I covered my mouth with shaky fingers, stifling the sob that tried to escape.

My God, I'd done that to him. My fingers trembled, and tears filled my eyes, causing the print on the page to blur. I was almost the cause of him ending his life. Every toxic thing I'd said to him had been to try purging it from within, but I'd never thought about what he'd struggled with. And even after the first verbal attack, he'd returned and tried again. *Why?*

I wallowed in the past, working to figure out what was between us. That pull. It had been there even then, and it still was. I couldn't deny my need to go to him when he entered a room. It'd been the same back then yet different.

I folded the note carefully and placed it back where it'd been.

I closed his wallet in front of me. Slowly, I shut the door on the past and examined what was between us.

After a while, a small thread of hurt and anger returned. I had been guilty back then, but that didn't explain why he'd lied to me about his name. We had been different people back then. *Did he honestly think I would continue to make fun of him? Was he the one sending me the threatening notes?*

Yes, I'd called him terrible things. The worst had been mocking his stuttering, calling him stupid, and telling him to go away—for good. I was wrong in what I'd done, regardless of the boatloads of despair I'd been drowning in.

That was then, and this time, he'd come after me.

I was the stupid one. I hadn't recognized him, and I'd believed his lies. I even fucking liked him—and I slept with him.

I swiped my phone off my desk and stabbed at his number. He picked up on the second ring.

"Hey—"

He sounded happy. *Not for long.* I put every ounce of my anger into his name. "Shane."

"Shit."

CHAPTER TWENTY

SHANE

I stopped in the middle of the walkway to class, my phone gripped tightly in my hand and pressed against my ear. People moved around me. It was too public for the argument, but I had no choice except to engage with Winter.

She knows who I am. It was so messed up. Her finding out had been inevitable. Still, after last night—the first night in I couldn't even remember how long—it was the best fucking night of sleep I'd had in weeks. I couldn't tell her that, though.

"You're a liar." She growled the accusation.

I couldn't do this here. Too many potential witnesses were around, and after my recent encounter with the police because someone had said they'd overheard an argument between Luke and me, I couldn't take any chances. I pushed through people and ducked into the closest building, taking the stairs at a fast pace until I was in the basement. It was quiet and empty— precisely what I needed.

"You're a liar too," I fired back. "It wasn't an accident that you almost drowned. Your mom is a killer. She murdered your sister. And you lied about that."

"Are you kidding right now?" Her voice went up an octave. "You don't know what you're talking about."

"I know plenty." I matched her tone, anger licking up my spine in a line of fire. "Ever look on the internet? Your family history is splashed all over it. Hard facts."

"Really? Maybe we should dive into your past. I bet I'll find tons of stuff on you too."

"You can try." At least mine was an accident. Hers involved murder and even had rumors that she was responsible.

"At least I didn't sleep with someone under a false identity. Who the fuck does shit like that? Fuck you, Shane."

She hung up on me? I pulled my phone away from my ear and looked at the screen. *Goddammit!* That wasn't how I saw the day going, especially after our night together. I shoved my phone back in my pocket and raked my hands through my hair, relishing the pain as I tugged on the strands. She had me all turned around.

I'd thought she was different. That had been my first mistake —*no, the second.* I'd misjudged her when we were kids too. The problem was with me. *Fuck!* I took the stairs two at a time and slammed through the door. My phone buzzed again with an incoming call. I yanked it from my pocket and hit accept without looking at the number.

"Shane."

Great—Professor Elian. I didn't have time for her. "Stop calling me, Cindy." My day just went from bad to worse. *Screw classes.* I was skipping.

"You haven't been taking my calls."

"Because we have nothing to discuss. And don't you have a class to teach?" I needed her off my back.

"I miss you. Come to my office." Her voice turned raspy, urgent. "I'm free for the next hour."

"What don't you understand?" I couldn't be any clearer in

my delivery. Nothing about how I asked that was pleasant. "I'm not interested. Go find someone else to harass."

"Harass? That's how you're going to talk to me after all the things we did together?"

"It was sex. Something we mutually agreed upon. Casual, with no strings. That's over now. I'm no longer interested. So lose my number, and stay the hell away."

"That's not how this is going to go, Shane," she snapped, her teacher's voice coming in loud and clear. "I'm going to tell my husband about us."

At my SUV, finally, I got in and closed the door for some privacy to deal with her. "You'll lose your job."

"I don't care." That whiny desperation pierced through the speaker. "I miss you. I want us to be together."

"I'm sorry you feel that way, but I don't. I meant it when I told you we were through last time." I switched the call to the speaker and pried my fingers from my phone before I cracked it.

"You pursued me!" she shouted. "You started this. What's your mom going to think when I tell her that?"

My head thumped against the headrest, and I closed my eyes. *Fuck me.* I'd known she was friends with my mom. Not good friends, more acquaintances, but still. The way Cindy had come on to me with her low-cut shirts and how frequently she'd touched my arm, shoulder, or stomach had made all that go out the window.

"I won't give up."

She'd gone from needy to desperate to angry and finally to an eerie calm that I did not like. "You're psycho."

She laughed. "This is because of that girl."

"I don't know what you're talking about." But something pricked my awareness about Cindy's unstable, or desperate, state of mind and what that could mean for me. "It's not because of anyone else. My decision to end our fling is because I'm no longer interested in you."

"That girl you spent the night with is not good for you. She's a killer."

Red flags went off all over the place. "How do you know where I spent the night?"

"I know everything about you."

I could picture her satisfied smirk as she leaned back in her office chair. "So, you're a stalker." I hung up. I couldn't talk sense into her. She just needed to find someone else to obsess over, and I hoped that would be soon.

My phone pinged, and I was almost afraid to look. The text was from Joe asking if I'd gotten the money. I shut off my phone.

I couldn't deal with people right then. Thane wasn't the place to be to get away from everyone. I hit the Start button and put my SUV in gear, then backed up, and after exiting the parking lot, I headed toward Mom's house. It was early enough that she might not have gone to sleep yet after her shift.

With the music cranked high, I drove home, my mind swirling with everything that had happened. Cindy didn't matter. I couldn't see her crazy amounting to anything. She would find another poor sucker to seduce. Not that I was a sucker, it had been a mutually gratifying situation. Until it wasn't.

Joe... I didn't want to unpack the stress around him texting me. The business he wanted to start, the second chance at being the dad he had never been, was for another day.

Winter was another issue. She'd gotten under my skin —again.

Last night had been incredible. Once would never be enough. But I couldn't see a way past her reaction to learning my real name or that I'd lied to her. She'd lied too. I couldn't forget about that. Then there was the plan I'd concocted to get back at her, but goddamn, one touch, and I craved more. I didn't know how she'd found out about me. It wasn't a stretch that someone had seen me with her and that was how she'd learned my name.

There wasn't much traffic, and I got to Mom's faster than I'd thought I would, which was good. After pulling into the driveway, I parked then rounded my car to unlock the front door. I didn't call out in case she was already asleep.

The clink of silverware against glass led me to the kitchen, and I found her loading her plate into the dishwasher. She still wore her scrubs, and her dark shoulder-length hair was in a haphazard bun.

"Mom."

She jumped then whirled, hand over her heart, bracing herself against the counter with her other one. "Shane. You scared me half out of my mind."

"Sorry." I hugged her.

Her eyes narrowed when I pulled back, and she scanned my face. "Why aren't you in class? Did something happen?"

"Just a bad morning." I forced a grin.

She didn't need to know everything. Mom always shouldered more than she should with Phoenix and me.

"How is school going?"

"Good. I'm managing better with classes now that football is over. We still have workouts and stuff."

"What about the incident between you and Luke Green?" She sat beside me at the kitchen island, her hand resting on my forearm. "I still think you should talk to someone. What happened was a terrible accident, and I know you're struggling."

"I'm fine." That was the last thing I wanted to rehash. "I don't need to talk to anyone. And Grandad is helping me with the legal stuff."

She was quiet for a second, seeing more than I wanted her

to. "Please talk to me, honey. Are you okay?" Then her eyes widened. "Is Aspen?"

I was such an idiot. I'd forgotten Phoenix had rushed his wife to the hospital closest to the university just yesterday under a false alarm. I grabbed onto the topic change like the lifeline it was. "Things are fine with Aspen. But you know she's having a hard time taking it easy. That's driving her out of her mind."

Mom smiled, her eyes crinkling at the corners. "Yeah, she doesn't seem like one to lie around."

I snorted. "She isn't, so Phoenix wants the rest of us to keep tabs on her when he's not there. She's been known to lift those surfboards she paints instead of waiting for someone else to do it for her."

"That's what Phoenix told me, too, but are you sure you guys have it covered? I can try to get some time off."

"We're good." There were enough of us. If I couldn't help, then our cousins or their girlfriends would. "Save your time off for when the baby comes. I'm sure they'll need a lot of help."

"I can't wait. I checked in with Phoenix late last night. He seemed good, but I'm sure it's wearing on your brother. It's good he's got you to help him."

I gave her a close-lipped smile. I hadn't been much help lately, and I felt like shit about it. I would have to make it up to him without him discovering my mess with Cindy, Joe, and now Winter. And in the back of my mind, on a horror reel, was Luke. I couldn't shake that memory or the guilt if I tried.

"Do you want some breakfast?"

Her words thankfully jerked me back to the present. "Maybe just an apple."

She took one out of the fridge, washed it, and handed it to me. I didn't have much of an appetite, but I took a bite and chewed before I asked her the thing I'd wanted to when she'd been working a double shift. The same day I'd found out at Grandad's that new evidence had come out against me.

"Do you remember when I was in fifth grade and school was kinda... difficult?"

"Do you mean when you and Phoenix started sleeping in the same room again for a while?"

Huh, I'd forgotten about that. That had been so my brother could make sure I wouldn't do anything to hurt myself. Having a twin was on a whole other level. We knew things about each other without even having to say a word. That was also why I wanted to avoid the meeting with our group he had scheduled later about taking shifts with Aspen so she wasn't alone. I couldn't avoid it, but I wanted to. He would know something was up without me saying anything.

"Ah, it was around that time. Do you remember a girl who drowned and one who almost did too?"

"Yes, it was terrible. The whole town went to the funeral. Their mama was a drug addict who pushed the little girls into the lake. The one who died was Cole's age, and the other was in your grade."

Everyone from my school went? "Why didn't I know about it?"

"Oh, honey. You were going through all that stuff with that bully at school, and your doctor didn't think you should be involved or know too much. So, we didn't talk about it."

I could see her point. "What else do you know?"

"Not much. Or not much more than what they showed on TV and in the papers. The mom was pretty normal when the girls were young. After her husband died, she started doing drugs, and it went to hell after that."

"Did you know their mom?" She could have, especially if she had a drug problem and got rushed to the ER.

"I did but not very well. When you boys were in preschool up until first grade, I think, you were in a playgroup with them and Cindy Elian's kids. But that was before Cindy and her husband started having problems. Last I heard, she hadn't gotten a divorce, so they must have resolved things. She teaches at Thane, but you might not cross paths with her. She's an art teacher."

Holy fuck. What Cindy had said about Mom finding out suddenly made sense. But I doubted it would have the effect she wanted. Mom would be furious at her mostly.

"The group fizzled out after Katrina's husband died. She closed herself off. Cindy had her own things going on with her husband cheating on her, and I was trying to get Joe to pay child support—or at least come spend time with you boys."

I snorted. "That didn't go well. I'm sorry, Mom."

She shook her head, a flash of anger darkening her eyes and pinching her lips. "That's not on you or your brother. Ever. Joe is Joe. And I know he wants a chance to get to know you now, which is your decision. I just... I don't..."

"It's all right, Mom. I know who raised me. Even though he's trying to have a relationship, it doesn't take away from everything you've done for us."

She waved her hand in front of herself. "Forget about that. I got sidetracked. Why did you want to know about what happened to the Patten family? It was so long ago." A shadow crossed her face.

I didn't want to lie to her. "I've been seeing Winter."

"What?" She jumped up from her seat at the island. "You need to stay away from that girl. Promise me, Shane. She was a mean little one, in case you've forgotten."

I hadn't forgotten. And I suspected some of that meanness was still inside her, based on our conversation that morning.

"That's not everything." Mom's eyes narrowed. "A rumor has always floated around that Winter was the one who pushed her sister, Summer, into the water."

Shit. I leaned back in my chair. I didn't know what to believe.

CHAPTER TWENTY-ONE

WINTER

I shook from how angry I was at Lan—*no, Shane. He was using me. But why?* I was such a fool. I'd even had sex with him. My stomach churned. I had been horrible to him as kids, but I couldn't think about that because I was humiliated, a joke in his eyes. I was sure of it. And even with all of that, I still wanted him.

What's wrong with me?

Do I have no self-respect? With a huff, I tried to leave it all behind me and got ready for classes. He wouldn't take that away from me. Mr. Big Shot football player could go to hell. I was there to stay, and that meant no more seeing him.

It couldn't be that hard. I was an art student. He wasn't. Our paths didn't have to cross. So I was good.

Except the coffee shop where I worked on occasion. It was time to make a call and put an end to my employment there. Then I was covered.

After convincing myself of all that, I took a shower, dried my hair, then got dressed and ready for class. Mine wasn't until eleven. I liked the course, just not as much as I'd thought I would. Professor Elian was friendly and overly helpful. I knew the other students loved her, but I got a weird vibe. I had no idea why.

I double-checked my messenger bag and noticed a folded paper on the floor. Someone had slipped it under the door. I unfolded it, dreading what it could be with each paper crinkle.

The world is going to know you killed Summer.

It was one line, but that was all it took for the room to spin around me. My knees buckled, and I sank into my desk chair. *It mentions Summer by name.* I couldn't tear my eyes from the single typed sentence.

My mind was splintering. I crumpled the paper and threw it in the trash. My breath pushed from my lungs too fast, and I panted, my heart racing a million miles a minute. Black spots crowded my vision, and I blinked furiously. I had to get control of myself. I dropped my head between my legs and focused on slowing my breathing.

It took a while, but I managed to calm down and not pass out or throw up. Logic trickled in slowly. Whoever that was—possibly Shane—could've read one of the numerous articles and gotten Summer's name that way. That made sense.

Brooke and my therapist had thought it was a good idea. Confronting parts of my past. It wasn't. I could see that now. *I shouldn't be here.* And I would leave, though I needed my scholarship and I hated disappointing my foster family.

But I never would have hurt my sister. We had just been trying to survive. After our dad died, it'd been a sick game of chance with our lives. *Would we eat that day? Would we have to hide from whoever Mom had in the apartment? Would we have to hide from her?* Nothing about my childhood had been good. Trying to reconnect, to remember, had been stupid.

I continued to focus on controlling my breath. It helped. Part of me was so glad Piper wasn't there to witness everything. We were talking more, becoming friends again, but we weren't close enough that I would share any of this with her. And my foster brother. I wanted to call him, and I still might. But not then. Not when I was so raw from that one horrifying accusation. I had not hurt my sister. I was sure of it. There was no way.

The longer I sat at my desk, the better I felt. For some unknown reason, someone—and I bet it was Shane—was playing a prank on me, a very mean one.

My phone buzzed, and I glanced at it. I didn't recognize the number, but I gathered who it was from the message. Landon —*no, Shane.* I needed to remember his real name and what a liar he was. The number was probably his real one, the other just a phone he used for his nefarious lying. He'd texted that he wanted his wallet back.

Asshole. I wished I could throw it out the window and tell him where it was—if he could get to it before someone else picked it up and he never saw it again. But I couldn't. I wasn't that girl. Not anymore.

I responded that I would meet him at the back exit once he messaged that he was there. It would be on my way to my art class then. And that would be the last time I ever saw him because I was done. No matter how mind-blowing the sex had been, I wanted nothing to do with him.

My heart hurt because I could've easily fallen for him. It would've been the first guy I'd ever loved. Thank God I'd found out what a lying asshole he was before that had happened.

I headed downstairs as soon as I saw his responding text that he was there. My hand shook with anger as I pushed open the door. It was sunny out, and I blinked against the bright light.

The hairs on my arms and the back of my neck stood as awareness rippled over me. Something wasn't right. Shane wasn't there. No one was. I felt a presence behind me. Someone grabbed the side of my head and slammed it into the doorjamb. Stars exploded behind my eyes, and my knees buckled. I tried to turn and screamed as a sweet-smelling cloth covered my mouth.

I reacted, struggled, tried to dislodge the cloth pressed firmly against my lips. An arm banded around my waist, pulling me back against something solid. My body grew heavy. Darkness converged around the edges of my vision, but still, I fought, digging my nails into the person who held me.

The more I tried to kick and scream, the weaker I got, until everything went black.

CHAPTER TWENTY-TWO

SHANE

I decided to spend the night at Mom's house and left in the morning feeling a little more centered after hanging out and talking with her.

Mom's final words about Winter bugged me more than I let her know. *Why would anyone think she killed her sister? Winter could be downright evil—I was privy to that knowledge when I was younger—but would she kill her sister?* No. I couldn't see that, not from the girl I'd gotten to know a little better this year.

Traffic was light as I drove to Thane. I couldn't miss another one of my classes and should make it on time. I cranked the tunes and increased my speed to five over the limit. So many things weighed on me—Joe, Grandad, and of course, Winter. And the pending arrival of Phoenix and Aspen's baby.

I moved over a lane and passed a slower car. It was hard to believe that in a month and a half, I would be an uncle. That little girl had no idea what kind of family she was about to be born into. We would spoil her and never let her date when she got older. No one would mess with her.

Good thing it was Phoenix and not me who'd gotten an instant family. He knew what he wanted and always had—to play in the NFL. And he was good enough to go in the first round of the draft. Adding a wife and kid would be challenging, but if anyone could succeed, it was Phoenix. I was so proud of my brother and hoped he knew it.

If that had happened to me, it could have been with Tracey—though I'd been aware of her gold digger ways, despite how I'd played it with my family—or worse, Professor Elian. I cringed at the reminder of the crazy I would have to deal with.

The cars around me slowed, and I glanced in my mirrors to see why. Two squad cars with lights flashing tore down the highway directly behind me. Turn signal on, I moved over a lane. They followed. Alarm spiked in my bloodstream, sending a jolt of tingles down to my hands as I gripped the wheel tightly. *What do they want?* I'd done nothing wrong.

One of the cop cars swerved and got in front of me, decelerating. I slammed on the brakes to avoid a collision. A fleeting thought ran through my mind that I wouldn't be able to sell my SUV if I got in a wreck. It was stupid. I had much bigger things to worry about. With a flick of my fingers, I pulled over to the shoulder. The cops sandwiching me followed until we came to a complete stop. I put my SUV in park. Leaning forward slightly, I went for my wallet but found my pocket empty. *Shit.* It wasn't there. *Goddammit.* I must have left it at Winter's.

No driver's license. I was so fucked.

Whatever happened, I wouldn't take a chance and lean over to get my insurance card in case they thought I had a weapon in the glove compartment. I didn't, but damn, it wasn't good.

I lowered the window, my gaze volleying between the squad car in front and the car visible in my mirrors parked behind me. Car doors opened, and I stayed still with my seat belt on.

I rubbed clammy palms along my jeans. No way would I be getting out of the ticket they would give me due to driving without my license. It wasn't what I needed. And I'd had enough of the police station to last a lifetime.

Guilt pierced me at that last thought. Luke lurked in the back of my mind at all times, how one mistake on my part had ended his life. *He was messed up, but who was I to be his judge, jury, and executioner?* It was a habit from high school I had to break. Something I'd learned the hard way. *But have I grown at all from it?* No. I hated to admit it, but with how things had played out with Winter, what I wanted to do, that told me I hadn't. *I need to be better.*

I snapped back to the present. My gaze alternated from the car in front to my mirrors to see what was happening behind me. I watched as cops jumped out of their vehicles, guns trained on me. I flattened my hands on the dash. *What the fuck is going on?*

"Shane Bennett?" The cop behind me growled his question.

The officer stood at my open window, his hand resting on the butt of his gun. He had dark-brown hair cropped close, a slightly hooked nose that was too big for his face, and alert eyes locked on me with an intensity that said everything he wasn't—accusation. I was guilty of something. *But what? Were the Greens involved?*

"Yes, I'm Shane." I didn't offer an excuse. I wasn't speeding excessively, which made the dread sit heavier in my gut as to why so many of them had pulled me over. "Is there a problem, Officer?" There was no reason to have one until he asked for my license and registration.

"I need you to step out of the vehicle. Hands where I can see them," the same guy commanded.

I wanted to argue. But things would have gone from bad to worse, so I complied. With slow, precise movements, I unbuckled my seat belt and opened the door.

As I followed the direction, I noted how the cars passing us on the highway slowed, gaping to see what idiot was being arrested. It was a fucking nightmare, and I was getting PTSD flashes from when they'd come and arrested me at Mom's house for Luke's death.

Hands raised to my shoulders, palms facing forward, I stood towering over the officer, my shoulders far broader than his.

"Step around to the back of your vehicle." A muscle leaped in his jaw, and his eyes narrowed.

I did as he said, not liking the heavy tension in the air. Something was going down, and I had no clue why I seemed to be under suspicion. "What's this about?"

"Hands behind your head."

"What's going on?" Beads of sweat edged my hairline. I hadn't done anything—*or nothing new.* I tensed, my gaze darting from one officer to the next.

The cop reacted. I realized too late that he'd read my body language as a sign of aggression. I was pulled around the back bumper of my SUV and told to lie down face-first. My hands went to the concrete, tiny stones and glass biting into my palms. When I was in the position they wanted with my ankles crossed, my hands were yanked behind my back and secured.

I turned my face to see what they were doing. I hardly noticed how the small stones pressed uncomfortably into my cheekbone. I lay there watching as the doors on my SUV were yanked open. It didn't take long.

The two officers from the front car had finished whatever search they were performing inside the front and back seats. It gave me a modicum of hope because I had nothing to hide. I didn't do drugs, and kept nothing incriminating in my car.

Hauled to my feet, I stood still as they popped the back of the Range Rover and yelled to another cop. "She's not in here!"

She? I had no clue what they were talking about. "She who? What's going on?"

They ignored me. After reading my rights, the same cop shoved me into the back of the squad car. I had to duck low. My head almost hit the ceiling, and there was barely room for my knees. It was bullshit.

The cop who'd shoved me into the back of the squad car held up a clear plastic evidence bag. My wallet was inside. "We know you took her. You dropped your wallet."

"Who?" I had a bad feeling it was a setup.

"If you tell us where she is, things will go a lot easier for you."

I needed to hear him say her name, though I already knew. Holy fuck had she played me. "Who are you talking about?"

"Winter Patten."

Ready to find out what happens between Shane and Winter?
To find out, continue reading the Hidden Valley Elite series
with Wicked Ends

https://www.islavaughnauthor.com/books

Keep up with Isla's releases by joining her newsletter:
https://bit.ly/IslaVaughnNewsletter

If you enjoyed reading WICKED GAMES as much as I did
writing it, I hope you'll consider leaving a review.

ABOUT THE AUTHOR

Isla Vaughn is the author of the Hidden Valley Elite series. Her romance books are full of complex characters, strong alpha males, and the fierce women who bring them to their knees. When not writing, she can be found daydreaming about owning a beach house, reading, or drinking too much coffee.

You can find her at:
https://www.islavaughnauthor.com

Subscribe to Isla's newsletter for cover reveals, book announcements, and giveaways:
https://bit.ly/IslaVaughnNewsletter

facebook.com/author.IslaVaughn

instagram.com/islavaughnauthor

goodreads.com/islavaughn_author

tiktok.com/@islavaughnauthor

twitter.com/IVaughn_Author

ALSO BY ISLA VAUGHN

Hidden Valley Elite Series

Savage Start

Savage Lies

Savage Truth

Brutal Days

Brutal Nights

Cruel Start

Cruel Hate

Cruel Love

Wicked Games

Wicked Ends

9 781951 919535